THE INCREDIBLE WILLIE SCRIMSHAW

DICK CATE

ILLUSTRATED BY CAROLINE HOLDEN

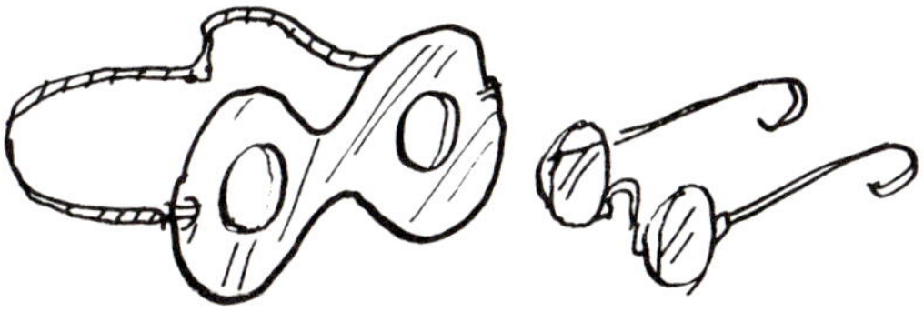

A & C BLACK · LONDON

To Phil Marshall
for being a real fan

First published 1991 by A & C Black (Publishers) Limited
35 Bedford Row, London WC1R 4JH

ISBN 0 7136 3316 6

A CIP catalogue record for this book
is available from the British Library.

Filmset by August Filmsetting, Haydock, St Helens
Printed in Great Britain by St Edmundsbury Press, Bury St Edmunds, Suffolk.

ONE

Trouble

If you'd seen Willie Scrimshaw coming out into the playground of Brick Street school that morning you would probably have thought: *What a squit he looks!*

And there you would have been right.

Skinny, undersized, *and* wearing jam-jar specs, he looked the sort of kid who couldn't beat the skin off a rice pudding.

For a moment he seemed to look vaguely round the yard. But in fact he was looking for one particular girl. Her name was Sally Mow, and he saw her almost at once, up at the top end of the yard, talking to Arnold Buttermouth.

He was glad somebody was talking to Sally: but sorry it had to be Arnold.

In Willie's opinion Sally Mow was the best-looking girl in the universe. He just knew she'd be a TV star one day, probably advertising something like wholemeal bread. All week he'd been hoping to partner her when they walked down to the Swimming Complex for the heats, but so far he hadn't managed it.

For one thing, Miss Minsky didn't approve of boys. *Rats and snails and puppy-dogs' tails* she said they were made of. She wouldn't allow them to sit next to girls in her class, or even walk with them down to the Complex. "Girls to the front, boys to the rear!" she'd said every time they set off.

For another, Sally seemed to prefer Arnold Buttermouth, who had tints in his hair and always got the spare milk because his mam was a teacher at Willie's school and she said he was a growing lad. (She seemed to be right because he'd grown a foot taller than anybody else in Miss Minsky's.) Every time he played *Kum-bah-yah* in assembly, some girls swooned on the gym mats and had to be revived by Mrs Dalrymple and her tin of Elastoplasts.

Willie pretended to remove a fly from his eye as he glanced up the yard again. Arnold was pointing up at the sky now. He'd got a telescope for his birthday and last weekend had discovered three new planets. He was probably pointing one of them out to Sally now. She seemed really interested. Arnold's brilliant teeth flashed – giving Willie a sudden pain in the head – and Willie had a terrible premonition of the pair of them getting married one day.

"Do thou, Sally Mow, spinster of this horrible parish, take Arnold Buttergob to be thy awful wedded husband?" the vicar was just saying. Sally didn't reply at once. Arnold was looking dead smirky. Then Sally said: *"Not on your Nelly!"* and the vicar looked flabgustipated. *"I beg your pardon?"* he said. *"Did you say* NOT ON YOUR NELLY?*" "I did,"* said Sally. *"Then who* do *you wish to marry, young lady?"* asked the flabgustipated vicar and Sally turned round to look at the back of the congregation where Willie was sitting. Her lips parted and she was just about to utter the magic words when somebody bawled them in his ear:

"WILLIE SCRIMSHAW!"

It was his best pal, Shrimp Salmon, the smallest kid in Miss Minsky's. "You daydreaming again, Willie?" he said. "I've been shouting at you for five minutes. Want a game of football?"

"Okay," said Willie, who often dreamed of playing for Muckyford United.

"I had a right funny adventure last night," Shrimp told him as they threaded their way down the yard, passing the ball between them. "You know Mandela flats they built ten years ago and now they're pulling down?"

"What about them?" said Willie, carefully dribbling the ball round a group of skippy-roping girls, so as not to spoil their fun.

"I was scratting around down there last night

and I heard this noise so I thought I'd investigate."

Willie smiled to himself because although Shrimp was a titch, he really fancied being a detective one day.

"Three big lads in there," said Shrimp, taking his position as goalie against the bike-shed wall. "They had this ghetto-blaster on right loud."

"What's funny about that?" asked Willie as he placed the ball ready for a kick. "I thought that's what ghetto-blasters were for?"

"I know," said Shrimp. "But they all had headphones on."

"Oh, aye?" said Willie. "What's funny about that?"

As he paced back from the ball he glanced up the yard: Sally was still listening to Arnold. Willie turned away. *This brilliant young striker is about to open the score for Muckyford!* he muttered as he began his run-up.

"But their headphones weren't plugged in," said Shrimp. "In other words, they were listening to nowt."

Willie shot for goal and hit a big girl half a mile off up the backside. She whirled round – obviously her pride had been hurt – but when she saw who it was she chucked the ball back, almost smiling.

"Sorry," said Willie. "Beg your pardon."

"It's okay, Willie," said the big girl. "I know you wouldn't do a thing like that on purpose. You're too much of a gentleman."

Most kids at Brick Street liked Willie Scrimshaw. If anybody was upset he was sure to offer them one of his mints, and he was always helping folk. It wasn't only folks he was nice to, either. He always spoke to next door's cat on his way to school, and he had only to see a worm risking life and limb on the pavement on a hot day and he'd move it somewhere safer. He looked round the yard to see if there was anybody he could help now, but unfortunately there didn't seem to be.

Though he could see that might not last.

Mr Miley, the headmaster, had just tottered out clutching on to his teacup for support. He wasn't a bad old codger, just a bit past it. All he thought about nowadays was Early Retirement and his timeshare villa in Portugal. He hadn't a clue what was going on around him.

And the trouble was, Nigel Bodger – a big boy in the top class – had just bounced into the yard with a particularly loony look in his eye.

"Why should they listen to nowt?" asked Willie as he dribbled the ball goalwards. *Scrimshaw beats one man, two men, three men,* he muttered under his breath. *Can nothing on earth stop this brilliant young dribbler?*

"Another funny thing was, they were all wearing masks," said Shrimp.

"Masks?" said Willie as he tripped over his own big feet and came down a whomper near the goal.

Shrimp helped him up. "Definitely a penalty, Willie," he said.

"Fair enough," said Willie.

He balanced the ball on a crisp packet and walked back ten paces. For some reason Nigel seemed to be heading for Sally Mow. Willie wondered why. Nowadays she hadn't any friends, not since some clot had called her Smellygrub down at the Swimming Complex. Since then folks had been avoiding her, some holding their noses and saying "Poo!" Still, thought Willie, she'd probably be all right with Arnold to protect her.

And now, William Scrimshaw, probably the best striker in the world ever to advertise Krogenpop Lager, is about to take the penalty that could win Muckyford the cup, muttered Willie as he rushed towards the ball like a professional and drew his foot back to kick hard.

"Mickey Mouse masks," said Shrimp – and Willie fell flat on his back, the ball stayed where it was, and the crisp packet headed for goal for a couple of yards, then gave up the ghost.

"Mickey Mouse masks?" said Willie, picking himself up.

"Well, one were Mickey Mouse and the other were Minnie, and the third lad were – who's that on telly with big teeth always frightening folk?"

"Prime Minister?" said Willie.

"No. Whatsisname? Count Dracula. You okay, Willie?"

"Champion," said Willie as he dusted down the new trousers that his mam had just bought at the Co-op. She'd play heck if he muckied them.

"They just sat there listening to nowt for ages," said Shrimp. "They turned up the volume till it were right loud, then started walking round with their masks on. Then a right funny thing happened. When they were leaving, they saw me and grabbed hold of me, and guess what they did, Willie?"

"Ask me another," said Willie.

"Minnie Mouse said he hated all little kids, so then Mickey – who seemed like the boss – ordered them to take me up to the top floor and hang me on a hook by my trousers. He didn't come up, he just stayed down below and watched. I think he thought I was scared of heights. But I'm not."

Willie nodded. He knew that was true. Yesterday, when Shrimp had won his diving heat from the top board he'd looked as cool as a little cucumber. Not like Willie had felt a few minutes before.

"They just left me dangling there, in suspense, like," said Shrimp. "You should've seen Mickey's eyes. It was as if he really hated me."

"What a funny do," said Willie. He looked up the yard and saw Nigel Bodger pushing Sally backwards. Arnold Buttermouth, his neck stretched out like an inquisitive giraffe's was still gazing up at the sky. His mam was always telling them in assembly what a go-getter Arnold was and Willie wondered if three new planets a week wasn't enough for Arnold.

Meanwhile, Sally Mow was in danger . . .

"Back in a tick, Shrimp," Willie called over his shoulder.

"Where you going?"

But Willie didn't reply. He was already on his way. *Bold Sir William Scrimshaw, his sturdy charger by his side, leapt astride his faithful buckler* thought Willie (who wasn't red-hot on detail) *and galloped to the rescue.*

And if you'd seen him galloping through the crisp packets, you would probably have thought: *What can a squit like that do about it?*

But there you would have been wrong.

TWO

A Damsel in Distress

It was typical of Sally Mow to be still grinning and bearing it, thought Willie, even though Nigel Bodger was shoving her around.

She and her mam (and baby Christine) were a one-parent family and had a hard job to make ends meet, but none of them ever complained. A lot of Sally's clothes were faded and second-hand, though they were always washed clean and pressed neatly. But when whoever-it-was had shouted out, "Smelly-grub's in the pool! Everybody out or you'll get poisoned to death!" a lot of daft kids had swum to the side and laughed at her. Sally hadn't seemed to mind, though Willie noticed she came last in her heat, so like him, she wouldn't be in the finals tomorrow; he was beaten by Arnold Buttermouth who had a ten-yard start because his mam said he had a bad cold.

In any case, Sally still had a chance of winning the Councillor Allgob Genuine Imitation Silver-Plated Trophy for Special Effort. For weeks she'd spent every spare minute knitting extra-solid ear-muffs – you couldn't have heard a brass band through them – which she sold for twenty-five pence a pair. She'd sold loads of them and had only one pair left. Willie would have bought them himself, if his dad hadn't stopped his pocket-money, again. But he *had* given her his very last penny and now she had ten pounds and a penny in her bag (Willie liked to think the extra penny was his).

It was all part of Councillor Allgob's scheme to raise money for Endangered Animals. Councillor Allgob had been Mayor of Muckyford for donkey's years now and people said he had a heart of gold, but they usually said it with a yawn because they remembered his speeches. People dozed off in the middle of the mayor's speeches and woke up three weeks later to find he was still only at the beginning. Last year, during the elections, when his loud-speaker van came down their street, Willie and his dad had been watching the Krogenpop Lager Cup Final and by the time the mayor had finished his speech and driven off to plague somebody else, they'd both nodded off and missed three yellow cards, two goals and a sending-off.

Nigel Bodger was trying to grab Sally's shoulder-bag now.

Fortunately for Willie, Arnold Buttermouth still hadn't seemed to notice that Sally needed help, although he was standing quite near. His mam was always telling them in assembly what a genius he was, and she was probably right because he obviously couldn't see what was going on under his nose.

And now this promising young boxer from Muckyford steps into the ring, Willie muttered through a gap in his teeth as he drew near.

"I won't take anything out," Bodger was saying. "Just want a look."

"I wasn't born yesterday, Bodger," Sally said. Nigel made a grab and Sally backed away. "I only have to shout, Bodger, and Mr Miley'll hear," Sally said.

"Smiley wouldn't notice if the sky fell on his head!" said Nigel. "It'd be different if Wonky Watkins was on duty!"

He was right, Willie thought. Mr Watkins stomped around *looking* for trouble. He was right keen, especially on grammar and Miss Minsky. Last week he'd helped her to get her car started, but she hadn't even smiled as she drove off, even though he had successfully adjusted her tappets.

Nigel took a pace towards Sally. "Two quid'll satisfy me!" he said.

"Crack another one, Bodger!" said Sally, her back to the wall by now.

"Excuse me," said Willie, insinuating himself between them, "is summat up? Fancy a mint, Nigel?"

"No! Push off, lamebrain!" said Nigel.

"This idiot's trying to grab my charity money, Willie," said Sally.

"Shut your mush, Smellygrub!" said Nigel.

"That's not very nice, Nigel," said Willie. He knew Nigel wasn't a bad kid, really. Trouble was, he worshipped his big brother – Spodger Bodger – who went round the streets shouting 'MUCKYFORD U–NI–TED, MUCKYFORD U–NI–TED, WE'LL SUPPORT YOU EVER MORE!' and chasing cats. Willie thought that Nigel, left to himself, wouldn't be so bad, really. Just slightly stupid. "I think you ought to leave her alone, Nigel," said Willie.

"Feel this, scrag-end!" said Nigel, and he punched Willie hard in the belly. Willie went down.

Oh dear! Our plucky young champion is down! A foul blow just below the belly button has floored him! But can he possibly recover? Yes he can, folks!

Nigel stepped forward and grabbed once more for Sally's shoulder-bag.

"I really don't think you should do that, Nigel," said Willie, reappearing somehow between them.

"I have warned you, scrag-end!" said Nigel and punched Willie's chest.

Oh dear! A catastroscope here at Harringay Arena! The plucky young flyweight is down again! Can he possibly get up this time? Yes he can, folks!

"Stick your nose in this, Scrimshaw!" said Nigel as Willie once more bobbed up between him and Sally. This time he punched Willie hard on the nose.

Blood spurted. Willie went down on his knees. *Eight . . . Nine . . . Nine and a half . . .* He saw stars. Millions of them. His head was swimming (just like it had been yesterday on the high diving board). *Nine and three-quarters . . .* He managed to struggle to his feet and Nigel was just about to hit him again when the bell went for the end of playtime.

"Saved by the bell, Scrimshaw!" said Nigel. "You were lucky this time!"

"You okay, Willie?" asked Sally. "You look a bit

pale. You want a hand?" And then, the thing that Willie had been hoping for all week happened. Sally put her hand in his. Every time they'd walked down to the Complex, Mr Watkins had ordered all partners to hold hands as they crossed Cemetery Road because the undertaker's hearses came at you dark, fast and dangerous – like crocodiles, Willie always thought – especially if business was lively. Every time Willie had wished Sally was his partner, but he'd never been lucky enough. But now he was holding her hand. A small, cool, delicate hand: it brought a sudden flush of colour back to Willie's cheek. "You're looking better already," said Sally, withdrawing her hand. "You want my hanky? Your nose is all bleeding."

"I better not," said Willie as they started towards school.

"Here," said Sally. "Dab it on. Bit of blood never hurt nobody!"

As Willie pressed the hanky to his sore nose he noticed how faded and worn it was, but it had the beautiful fresh smell of washing-powder.

"Had a lovely playtime, children?" asked Mr Miley as they passed him.

"Champion, thanks sir," said Willie.

"That's the style," said Mr Miley, "schooldays are the happiest days!" He smiled down at them. He was always smiling nowadays. He had even smiled yesterday when he was on dinner-duty when there was that much noise that Miss Minsky had pretended she was overcome by it and borrowed Sally's leftover ear-muffs, just for a joke.

"There was no need to do that for me, you know, Willie Scrimshaw," said Sally as they went through the porch together. " I can stick up for myself."

"I know, Sal," said Willie. "Sorry about the blood."

"It'll easy wash out," Sally said, taking the hanky back. "You are daft, Willie Scrimshaw! Who do you think you are? A knight in shining armour?" She was only saying that because Miss Minsky went on about him always doing projects on Knights In Dayes of Olde (he'd only done sixteen so far). "Always imagining!" she scoffed.

That was true. He was always imagining damsels

in distress and dragons in need of slaying. Last night when he'd gone out to fill the coal bucket he'd opened the coalhouse door and seen all sorts in there: witches, dangers, visions. His dad had sent his mam out to see if he'd got lost.

"You're not a blinking prince!" Sally went on, as they went in Miss Minsky's.

It was funny she should say that. For the same suspicion had often entered Willie's mind. He sometimes seemed to remember a far-off time, a far-off place; highborn parents; a banqueting hall hung with shields that bore his family motto (it had two C's in it); the clash of swords, the neigh of noble steeds. All dreams, of course. Empty dreams. Or so he had always thought . . .

THREE

A Messenger From Outer Space

That night Willie started his seventeenth project, by coincidence entitled Knights in Dayes of Olde. He was just adding the final gobbets of blood to a picture of a good knight clonking a bad knight on the napper with one of those spiky things he couldn't remember the name of, and muttering *On thy knees thou scurvy varlet!* at the same time, when the whole house shook, rattled and rolled, and The Messenger from Outer Space descended into the bathroom.

"That you jumping on the bed with your new Co-op trousers on, Our Willie?" his mam shouted up from downstairs.

"No, Our Mam," Willie shouted back down.

"Well give over, and don't do it again!" she shouted back up.

"I humbly beg your pudding," said The Messenger from Outer Space as he stepped through the wall which separated Willie's room from the bathroom. Fortunately for The Messenger, Willie's sister, Darleen, had just vacated it (Darleen wouldn't half have given him a mouthful). "I would have been here earlier, only I was held up by major spaceworks on the Mars overpass."

He was small and bony with a sticking-out nose. All round him was a flickering blue light and when he flung up his left hand with great urgency, Willie naturally thought he needed to leave the room. He was about to point The Messenger back in the right direction when the creature shouted: ''Snow!''

''Pardon?'' said Willie.

''Snow, oh high and mighty one!''

''Snow?'' said Willie. ''Oh! I see what you mean! I think you've made a mistake, Mister. I reckon the word you're searching for is *Hail*.''

''We do not mack mistooks,'' said The Messenger. ''We are incoppable of it! You see this blue light all round me? That is my transmission light. The only way I could mack a mistook would be if this light was flickering, and it is not, for our technology is peefect.''

''But it *is* flickering,'' said Willie.

The Messenger looked down at himself. ''It is not,'' he said, looking up at Willie again. ''It must be a pigment of your imagination. But tim flees, and we must get down to bustiness! Know ye, that I come from a faraway planet, deep in space, to tell you of your birthright and your motion here on Earth. My name, sire, is Jeepio, The Official Bringer of Missages. Know ye, Willie Scrimshaw, that seven long mongs have possed since forst you left our galaxy -''

''Hang on!'' said Willie. ''Are you an advert for chocolate, Mister?''

The Messenger drew himself up to his full height – almost level with Willie's kneecaps – and stared up his long nose at Willie. Then he said in a haughty voice, ''Enough of this frivolity! Know ye, sire, that your name is not Willie Scrimshaw at all. Long mongs ago that name was chosen so that you could pass unnoticed among earthling creatures. Your true name is one of honour and renown."

"Flipping heck!" said Willie who had never reckoned much to Willie Scrimshaw as a name.

"Know ye, that you are of royal extinction," said Jeepio, "I am not just spoking through rose-coloured spictacles. You come from a nobble and illustrated family, which is why a gentleman of leisure was chosen as your earthly father and why you live in Balmoral Crescent, quite near to the Queen."

"Quite near to the Queen?" said Willie. "Balmoral Crescent's part of the Muckyford council estate. And nobody's ever called my dad a gentleman."

"He toils not, neither does he spin," said Jeepio, rather annoyed.

"Nobody spins round here now," said Willie. "All the mills are shut down. My dad's on the dole."

"We must not quobble over dovetails," said Jeepio. "Know ye, Willie Scrimshaw, that blue blood spurts through thy vines."

Willie was not as flabgustipated by this news as you might think: looking down at his blood on Sally's hanky as he handed it back in the playground he'd noticed it had a bluish tinge. Not exactly blue: but certainly blue-*ish*.

"Know also that your nobble father was an Obsblud of the First Order and your mother nothing less than an Inglenuke."

"Ecky thump!" said Willie.

"And that your name, oh high and mighty one, is Dingbat Bogholler!"

Willie had often imagined having an improved name. Nothing fancy. Arthur Truehart, Wayne Pewter, or just plain Frederick Steelsword would have done. But to be perfectly frank, Dingbat Bogholler had never once crossed his mind.

"Know also that you are a prince of a worrier race," said Jeepio, "which is why you are so tall."

"Tall?" said Willie.

"Almost a giant," said The Messenger, staring imperiously up at him. "You are surely not quobbling again? I hope not, your mudgesty. You are from the far land of Burp, a race of people wise, nobble, and respected throughout the seven universes. An all-poorful people. Invincible."

"Invincible, eh?" said Willie, who had somehow always fancied the idea of being invincible. "I suppose things are all quiet in Burp?"

"As a matter of fact, things have been very nosy lately," said The Bringer of Missages. "Much tribble with the Boggolots."

"Nosy?" said Willie. "How can you be having tribble with the Boggolots if you're invincible?"

"Simple, your mudgesty," Jeepio said, smirking up at him, "because the Boggolots are one stage more invincible than we are! Which is why your nobble father, fearing for your liff, sent you down here to this primitive planet. However, this is beside the pint. Whilst you are down here your motion in life is to help the earthlings, the so-called human beans."

"Beings," corrected Willie. "Beans come in tins. People eat them."

"People eat tins down here?" asked The Messenger incredulously. "Surely not, your mudgesty. Does it not hem their stimocks?"

"Never mind," said Willie. "How come if my motion in life is to help human beings you made me so puny? How come I have to wear jam-jar specs?"

All his life Willie had been forced to wear his

specs which were now heavily fortified with sticky-tape and butressed with pipe-cleaners. According to his mam they were already stuck on his nose when he'd arrived as a delightful surprise out of the blue at the Councillor Allgob Memorial Hospital, where she'd been taken in with a bad case of suspected wind.

The Messenger smiled a satisfied smile.

"I have been waiting for you to ask these questions. Your jam-jar spooks – as you so quaintly call them – are there not because you need them but to congeal the true power of your eyes, which have incredible powers. Like your punny body they are part of your disgust."

"Disgust?" said Willie.

"Gut hiffens! What is that nose!" said The Messenger.

"Nose?" said Willie, clutching his own nose protectively. He felt aggrieved, though hardly surprised. The nose he had was undoubtedly an offending article and since Nigel had womped it one it was looking particularly large and swollen. "It's the one you gave me," he said.

"Pudden me," said The Messenger, "I did not say noise, I said nose!"

"Oh! You mean nose!" said Willie, pointing at the bathroom wall. "Don't worry, that nose you can hear is only me dad running the bath next door. He believes in regular baths, me dad. He has one every year."

"Thank goodness for that!" said The Messenger, "it must be a relief for you all. Tick off your jam-jar spooks, your highness, and lick through that wall. What do you saw?"

At first Willie sawed nothing. But gradually his eyes adjusted, and he staggered back in a state of shock. "Ecky thump and black puddens!" he said. "It's me dad in the bath, wearing only his pipe! What a horrible sight!" he said, hastily replacing his specs.

"You will find, your mudgesty, that having incredible power is not all pleasure," said Jeepio with some satisfaction. "As with your eyes, so with your buddy. It too was designed to look punny for particular raisins. First, so that you would go unrecognised on earth. Second, so that you could squeeze into this. Lo and be healed!" he said as he held up what looked like a battered sports bag. He unzipped it, turned it inside-out, and took out:

a snazzy pair of underpants;

a pair of boots with suns and moons on them, plus matching gauntlets;

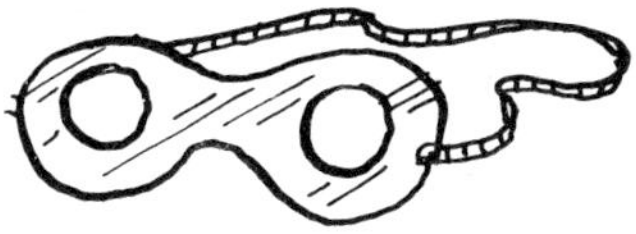

a silver mask like the one Willie had found in the bottom of a cornflake packet years ago (and lost a week later when his mam had her annual chuck-out); and a one piece suit made of green plasticky-looking stuff.

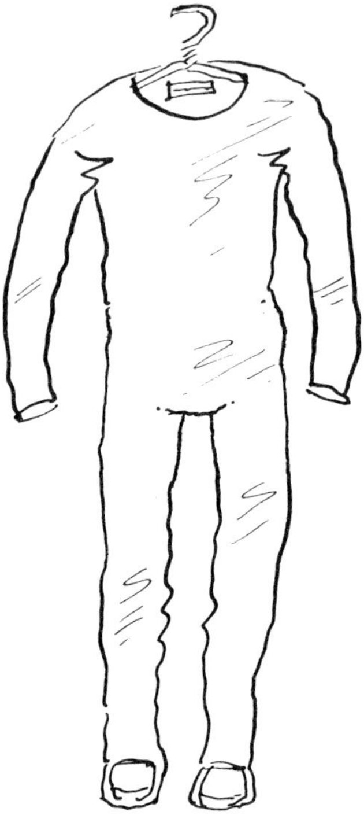

"Very nice," said Willy. "What is it?"

"Your worrier tunic," said The Messenger. "By itself it is nothing. But once your buddy is completely inside it, this suit will protect you against bullets, laser-rays, mortar bombs, radio-activity and acid ruin.

"Wow!" said Willy.

Also, once inside this suit, your buddy will expand to its true size, you will be all over muscles. You will be your true self, at last. Also, your bron will be gifted with amazing intencigell."

"That'll be nice," said Willie. "I've always wanted amazing intencigell."

"Most important, this suit will enable you to fly, to become all-poorful. Any damage must be repaired at once with the High Tech Repair Outfit located under the left armpit. Handwash only in lukewarm water, and avoid squeezing."

The Messenger adjusted a knob on his belt and began to sparkle.

"Fly?" said Willie doubtfully. "This – kit – will enable me to fly?"

"Once inside the suit it is simply a case of confidence," said The Messenger. "Mind over matter. Never forget that. It could save your loaf. If your courage fails, recite the names of your nobble and illustrated family: your Cousin Bravvoguts Slobsgod; Grandad Neagle who, never forget, held the banner at The Battle of Borts; Sickbert of the Flashing Blade; and not forgetting your Nobble Father. In moments of extremity, recite your family motto: *Coconuts conquers oil!* That will restore your fallen sparrots at once."

"*Coconuts conquers oil?*" repeated Willie. "You're sure that's right?"

"As I spok before, we never mack mistooks. Now I must goo. My dotties are perfumed! It is tim for my transmission. Excuse me, Prince Dingbat Bogholler! Snow and farewell!"

"Snow and farewell!" said Willie (who knew when he was beaten).

The Messenger shimmered bluely – reminding Willie of the time his dad had stuck his finger in the wall-socket to test if it was working (and it was). The whole house shook, causing dust from the bricks to seep out between the joins in the wallpaper, and The Messenger vanished through the ceiling.

"Is that you jumping on the bed again, Our Willie?" shouted his dad.

"No, Our Dad," said Willie.

"Well, give over this minute," said his dad. "You heard what your mam said. Don't you never listen to nobody nowadays?"

Willie listened till he could hear his dad playing quietly with his little rubber duck again. Then he held up his flying suit for inspection. It was crumpled and creased, he was sad to see, as if it didn't travel well.

Still, he thought, it was simply a case of confidence. Mind over matter. That was what The Messenger had told him.

Hastily he scrambled into the suit, then stepped into the snazzy underpants. He pulled on the zippy gauntlets and knee-length boots. Finally, being careful not to look bathroom-wards, he removed his jam-jar specs and put on his silver mask. He *did* feel more powerful.

At first when he looked at his wardrobe mirror he saw straight through it. (He could see his Banana-man T-shirt which he saved for best, and his pin-up of Vivien Cloggend, the Muckyford striker.) But gradually his eyes adjusted and he saw a small but incredibly powerful figure staring back at him, an all-over muscles one. He smiled, and saw that even his teeth were improved, almost as good as Arnold Buttermouth's now. The underpants were brilliant. Real bobby-dazzlers. He'd never seen anything like them in the Co-op. How he wished Sally Mow could see him now. She would probably swoon at his feet. Only the nose was the same. A long jutty-out thing that even the mask couldn't hide.

He could hear his dad letting the bath water out. Now was a good time to test his suit. He scrambled up on top of his wardrobe, taking care not to sit on George (a spider who resided up there), and a dead fly (which Willie had thrown up last week for George's lunch). It looked a long way down to the bed, but he had to try it. *Simply a case of confidence!* he reminded himself. *Mind over matter!*

He took off, whizzed twice round the ceiling light, almost clawed his Save the Whale map off the wall, and landed on the bed with a crash.

He heard his mam open the downstairs door.

"That you jumping on the bed again, Our Willie?" she shouted up. "I'm trying to concentrate me brains down here!" She was watching her favourite quiz programme *Money for Jam!* You only had to answer eighty-four questions, arrange them in the right order, and send off two thousand jam labels and you got a free fortnight in the South Pole. (Darleen was dying to go to the South Pole because it was the only spot on earth her best friends Sharleen and Marlene – who worked with her in the dole office – hadn't been to yet.)

"Sorry, Our Mam," Willie shouted down.

"Beds don't grow on trees, my lad!" she shouted up.

She slammed the door. The bath-water had run out now. His dad must be drying himself. Taking great care not to look through the bathroom wall, Willie tip-toed over to his window, opened it, and scrambled out onto the sill.

And now, he said to himself, *the moment the universe has waited for! The Incredible – the Invincible – Willie Scrimshaw, prepares for his maiden flight!*

FOUR

Dirty Plans Afoot

"What you do to him?" Spodger Bodger was asking his brother.

He was stretched full length on the sofa, his bovver boots poking over one end, his red-white-and-blue Mohican jutting over the other. As he half-listened to what his kid brother said, he was chewing on an apple and studying a book called *How To Bung Up Lifts*.

"So then I give him a fourpenny one up the hooter!" said Nigel proudly.

"Great!" chortled Spodger. "Then what'd he do?"

"Gorrup again," said Nigel.

"Gorrup again?" said Spodger. "You can't have lammed him hard enough. Scrimshaw's nobbut a weed!"

"I know that, Spodger, but you should see him. He's scared of nowt."

"He can't be scared of nowt!" said Spodger flinging his apple core at the cat, which sprang two feet in the air and landed almost in the coal bucket. "*I'm* the only one round these parts that's scared of nowt! Scared of nothink, me!" said Spodger. "This girl you were telling me about a minute back – her with all the money – what was her name again?"

"Sally Mow," said Nigel, "but *I* call her Smellygrub, because she stinks!"

"I like it! Smellygrub! Fruity one, that. Didn't know you was good at English, Nige! And she's got a load of money in that bag, has she?"

"Over ten quid. Tomorrow, she might win the Councillor Allgob Genuine Imitation Silver-Plated Trophy for Special Effort."

"Where you say she lives again?"

"Hope Street. What for, Spodger?"

"Never mind," said Spodger, who must have tired of his studies by now, for he flung *How To Bung Up Lifts* at the cat, which lifted off at ninety miles an hour and this time *did* land in the coal bucket (amusing Nigel and his brother no end). Spodger took a small object from his pocket.

"What's that, Spodger?"

"Amplifier," said Spodger, adjusting it with a screwdriver.

"What's an amplifier?"

"It makes things louder."

"Was that an amplifier you used the other night when you turned up the music and the cat shot up the chimney?'' asked Nigel, chortling and looking towards the cat, who was keeping her head well down in the coal bucket.

''You don't half catch on quick, Nigel!'' said Spodger.

''What for you keep wanting to make the music louder, Spodger?''

''Who says I want to make music louder this time? Did I say that?''

Nigel looked across at him admiringly. He was so smart, his brother.

''What *do* you want to make louder then?''

''Secret,'' said Spodger tapping the side of his nose. ''Big job.''

''What big job?''

''Never you mind. Between me and my mates.''

''Want any help, Spodger?''

''Not from useless little kids, we don't!''

''You going to chase cats again?'' asked Nigel.

''Don't be stupid!'' said Spodger. ''I told you, real big job. Half-inching!''

''Half-inching?''

''Rhyming slang. Mince pies – eyes. Butcher's hook – look. Half-inching –''

''Oh, yeah!'' said Nigel, ''I get it!'' (though he didn't really).

''Only we don't want you breathing it all over the neighbourhood. Trouble with you is, your mouth's too big,'' said Spodger. ''You'll read about it in the papers, anyroad. It'll be all over the papers soon enough. You'll see then how big your brother really is!"

"I know you're big, Spodger," said Nigel, "I know that."

It wasn't just his brother's Mohican and his combat boots Nigel admired. There were his tattoos, for instance. *And* the ring through his nose.

Spodger levered himself up from the sofa, stalked to the dresser and took a paper bag from the drawer. He looked inside to check the contents, then shoved it in his pocket.

"What's that?" asked Nigel. He was curious to know because he thought it might be a present for his birthday tomorrow.

"Just something I got from the Trick Shop."

"Trick Shop?" said Nigel, quite excited. "Something for me?"

"What you on about?" asked Spodger.

"It's me birthday tomorrow."

"Is it? Hard cheese! It's something to hide behind, if you want to know."

"Like a wall, you mean?" asked Nigel.

"You ever heard of a wall being in a paper-bag, Nigel?" said Spodger as he put a pair of pliers in his pocket. "Thick as two short planks, you are!"

"You going to go half-inching now?" asked Nigel.

"First I'm going to collect Noggin from work."

"Is he out of prison?" asked Nigel.

"Come out last week. It's a laugh who he's working for an' all now."

"Who?"

"Last sort of firm you'd expect. Then we going round for Sloworm."

"Bet Sloworm's not working!" said Nigel.

"He's on one of these stupid government schemes," said Spodger. "Making locks and keys. Thought we might as well take advantage. Get it?"

"Oh, yeah!" said Nigel (only, he didn't, again).

Just before Spodger went out he stuck the amplifier in his transistor and turned up the volume so high the cat flew out of the coal bucket and up the chimney for the second time in a week, only this time much faster.

FIVE

Stomper Chickens Out

"Hey up, Our Stomper, give over pulling!" said Sally Mow as he dragged her down Hope Street. He'd already broken one collar, and now looked set to break the new tartan one they'd just bought him. "Give over, you daft thing!"

Stomper had grey, distinguished-looking whiskers hanging down from his chollops, and everybody agreed he had a remarkably fine profile. His ambition in life was to marry Lovely Lucy, the police dog he was always seeing on the local news programme. Stomper was a big stroppy-looking dog who walked with a strut, a glint in his eye closely modelled on Clint Eastwood's, and grown men had been known to cross the road when they saw him approaching.

But he came to an abrupt halt as he turned into Gasworks View.

For leaning against the bus-stop were Mickey Mouse, Minnie Mouse and Count Dracula. And the moment Stomper saw them his legs came all over wobbly and the strut drained entirely from his paws.

Count Dracula he didn't mind so much. Mice, however, were a different kettle of fish: he seemed to remember an awful story his Uncle Hamish McKilt had once told him – a story about Mickey Mouse and a dog and a sausage-machine.

As Sally and Stomper drew near, Count Dracula dropped a fizzy-drinks can on the pavement. Sally picked up the can and put it in a litter-bin.

"You shouldn't drop litter," she said. "Litter's a sort of pollution, and pollution kills people. Miss Minsky's been telling us all about it."

"What do people do?" sniggered Mickey. "Trip over fag packets and break their necks?"

The other two laughed. Count Dracula turned his pockets out onto the pavement. "You can pick that up and all, if you like!" he jeered.

"Why are you all wearing them funny masks?" she asked them. "Are you waiting for a bus? The next one isn't till ten-past."

"Who said we were waiting for a bus?" asked Mickey Mouse.

"What *are* you waiting for, then?" said Sally.

"Waitin' for you, Smellygrub!" said Mickey Mouse. "Grab her!"

The other two grabbed her arms. Sally screamed but nobody heard her.

Everybody along Gasworks View was watching episode 156 of *Riches*, the awfully realistic soap-opera, in which Emilia-Anne was getting married in white for the fourteenth time, this time to the husband of her ex-friend, Martini Gorgeous, whose plane had mysteriously run out of petrol over the Gulf of Mexico after Emilia-Anne had filled up the fuel tank. So nobody saw Mickey Mouse snatch the lead from Sally and drag Stomper away from her. If it had been anybody else Stomper might have put up a fight. But not against Mickey Mouse. It was true he bared his teeth (like Clint Eastwood chawing on a cigar) and growled his Number One growl. But Mickey Mouse clearly wasn't scared of dogs, so Stomper rolled over on his back and gave in.

He felt so ashamed as he allowed himself to be tethered to some garden railings. He looked away, pretending not to hear Sally's cries for help. A tear fell from his Clint Eastwood-type eye, considerably dampening his distinguished-looking whiskers. He looked up the street instead, as if there was something to see, then turned his wonderful profile to the railings and wished he could die, grateful only for the fact that Lovely Lucy could not see him now in his moment of shame.

"Feels like a load of money in here!" said Mickey Mouse, who had grabbed Sally's shoulder-bag. "Thanks a million, kid!"

"That money's for the Endangered Animals Fund!" Sally shouted.

"I *am* an endangered animal!" laughed Mickey. "The Employment Office nearly offered me a job last week!"

"Can't we hang her up or summat, chief?" asked Minnie. "Like we did wi' that other little kid last night?"

"Okay," said Mickey. "Give us a lift."

And together they lifted Sally up and suspended her by the straps of her dungarees over the top of the bus-stop.

"Little kids should have better things to do than hang around the streets all night!" jeered Minnie. "Haven't you got a youth club to go to?"

"There isn't one round here, funny!" Sally shouted down at him. "Why don't you start one?"

"That's a laugh!" sniggered Minnie. "I hate little kids!"

And all three of them ran away, leaving Sally suspended on the bus-stop.

Sally screamed and screamed: but nobody heard her.

It was just coming up to the best bit in *Riches* when Emilia-Anne was sipping champagne from her slipper at the wedding reception on her yacht in the Bay of Acapulco, and looking at her fourteenth husband with eyes drippy as a soaking-wet spaniel's, while the sun sank in the west and an orchestra of a thousand baldy-headed fellers fiddled away like billio just out of sight of the camera. And naturally, nobody in their right senses living along Gasworks View was going to miss a second of that.

SIX

Here We Go! Here We Go!

Willie, meanwhile, was still preparing for his maiden flight.

Far below him, he saw the concrete floor of the back yard and his dad's long-johns swinging idly to and fro on the washing-line. Next door's cat was cleaning its paws on the outhouse roof and pretending not to notice him.

It all looked a blinking long way down to Willie.

Mind over matter, The Messenger had said. *Simply a case of confidence.* He'd also said *We never mack mistooks* (after, you will remember, macking several) and you can imagine how reassuring Willie found those words.

He eased his bottom forward slightly on the sill, and shut his eyes.

Here we go! Here we go! Here we go! he said to himself.

But he didn't go.

His mam came out into the yard to fetch a shovelful of coal and as she crossed back over the yard she glanced up and saw him.

"You finished your homework already, Our Willie?" she said.

"Yes, Our Mam."

"Your dad'll be going for the chips soon. You want a special or what?"

"Special, please Mam."

"Onion bhajis?"

"Pineapple rings," said Willie.

"Don't sit up there over long, Our Willie," she said.

"What for, Our Mam?"

"You might catch cold," she said, and she went back in and shut the door behind her. "You'll never guess what his lordship's up to now?" Willie heard her say to his dad. "Sitting on his window-sill, bold as brass."

"He wants to be careful up there," said his dad.

"What for?" she asked, after throwing some coal on the fire.

"If he leans back too far he could easy break the glass."

"I never thought of that," said Willie's mam. "By the way, he wants onion bhajis when you go down for the chips."

"I'll just watch this Regional Quarter Final of the All England Woofibix Left-Handed Tiddlewink Championship first," said his dad.

"By gum, that sounds interesting," said his mam. "I think I'll join you."

By straining his lugholes Willie could just hear the tiddles being winked as he looked out from his vantage point. The headlights of cars on the distant motorway flashed over the hillside as they rounded the corner from Uddersfax; the yellow streetlamps of Muckyford M.B.C. generously lit up every hill and valley, including the sheep baa-ing away on the tops.

Nearer to him, down in Cheap Street, Mr Shufflebotham was opening his fish shop for the night, and a terrible thought occurred to Willie: what if his teeth were destined never again to taste another of Mr Shufflebotham's fat greasy delicious chips?

Desist! thought Willie. *Verily, this is the way all scurvy knaves and varlets do think! It is now or never!* He wiggled his bottom forward until less than a centimetre still clung to the sill. Again he shut his eyes and said, *Here we go! Here we go! Here we go!* But still he didn't go.

It was all very well going on about confidence, he thought. But what if a mistook had been mad after all? He wondered if he should put off the whole thing until tomorrow. Or, better still, next year?

He looked down into the yard again. It seemed even further now. A breeze blew the top of his dad's long-johns open and an even more terrible thought occurred to him. What if, instead of landing on the outhouse roof or the concrete floor of the back yard, he ended up headfirst down his dad's long-johns? It seemed a fate worse than death. To take his mind off such an awful thought, Willie looked further afield, towards the Swimming Complex. He saw the red warning light at the very top of the Observation Tower blinking on and off to warn low-flying aircraft, and for some reason that reminded him of what had happened to him in the diving heats yesterday.

He'd been all right on the low board, and not so bad on the six-footer. It was on the top board that things had gone wrong for Willie. Shrimp had gone first. A near-perfect dive. Then it was Willie's turn.

It had taken him ages to climb up, and as he walked along the board it'd seemed terribly bouncy. There was a heck of a wind up there. The screams and cries of people far below him were faint and distant, as if from another land.

He had looked down for Sally by the poolside where he'd last seen her. She waved what he thought was a tiny red hanky (which turned out later to be a huge bath towel). He waved back, gently. He couldn't turn back now. Not with Sally watching. Sally would never turn back. She wasn't that sort. She wouldn't want him to, either. He remembered Nelson's signal to the Fleet, and prepared to do his duty.

When he reached the end of the board and looked down, he was amazed to see that the pool had shrunk to the size of a postage-stamp. It was possible he might even miss it and end up going through the roof of the Ladies Changing Rooms – *Sorry to drop in on you like this, missus!*

He didn't want to dive. But there are certain things in life you have to do, whether you want to or not. He had noticed Miss Minsky was watching him. Miss Minsky, who didn't reckon much to lads, who thought all men were cowards and bullies. "Never there when you really need them," she'd said yesterday. "And when they *do* turn up they offer you a box of chocolates as if that'll put matters right. But," she'd added, "there are some things in life more important than chocolates." There'd been a fiery look in her eye as she spoke.

And Willie had pressed his palms together. Shut his eyes. And leaned forward.

And that's what he did now. *Here we go!* he thought easing his backside the last millimetre forward on the sill. *Here we go! Here we go!*

And this time – reciting the names of his Cousin Bravvoguts Slobsgod; Grandad Neagle who, never forget, held the banner at The Battle of Borts; Sickbert of the Flashing Blade; and not forgetting his nobble father – he actually went . . .

At first he thought, Not so bad! I'm doing okay here!

It had been like that when he'd gone off the diving board. At first he'd kept himself beautifully straight, palms pressed together, toes pointing artistically backwards, the sort of thing Mrs Buttermouth and the other judges would be looking for. It wasn't till he was halfway down that he'd developed a slight wobble. Nothing to worry about at first, he'd thought. But as the water got nearer, the wobble developed from a slight wobble into a big wobble and then from a big wobble into a bigger wobble and then from a bigger wobble into a whopping wobble. And every time he tried to correct the whopping wobble, the whopping wobble got worse. Until three-quarters of the way down, when his legs had made their minds up to tip forward over his head. Four fifths of the way they were pointing in ninety-three different directions at once, and his arms were semaphoring messages for help . . .

. . . and that, funnily enough, was exactly what was happening now as he headed down speedily towards the left trouser-leg of his dad's long-johns . . .

SEVEN

Dark Deeds

After Mickey had cut a hole in the perimeter fence and all three had crawled through, Count Dracula looked round and said: "Isn't this the Swimming Complex? What we going to nick in here, S-"

"What did I tell you just before we set off?" snapped Mickey, cutting him short. "What did I tell you half an hour ago?"

Count Dracula angled his head in an effort to think.

"Can't remember, boss."

"Didn't I say not to mention our real names?" said Mickey, his eyes glinting angrily behind his mask.

"Oh, yeah! I remember now, Sp-"

"There you go again!"

Minnie Mouse giggled.

"Shurrup, you!" said Mickey. "You're nearly as bad as he is! Now listen, the pair of you. Brick Street kids are doing this charity thing tomorrow, trying to raise money for animals in this pool, and that's what we gonna nick."

"What we nicking the animals for, boss?" asked Count Dracula?

Minnie giggled. "He doesn't mean the animals," he said. "We're nicking the pool, you idiot!"

"We're *not* nicking the pool!" said Mickey. "It's the kids' money we're nicking!"

"Great!" said Minnie. "That'll show the little brats!"

"I *like* animals," said Count Dracula. "Especially dumb ones."

"You would!" said Mickey. "Now listen. Tomorrow, Minnie, your security firm will gather up the sponsor money and the takings from the side-shows and take it all to one room where that Miss Minsky is gonna count it. And you're certain there's a loudspeaker in that room? Am I right?"

"Right, chief," said Minnie, "but I just thought of something nasty. The room we're taking it to is right at the top of the Observation Tower. We had to carry Miss Minsky's school desk up there this morning. How we gonna nick the money from six flights up? We'll get nobbled."

"We won't get nobbled," said Mickey.

"But like I told you, chief, there'll be a police car parked at the bottom, right beside the lift, with three coppers in it and Lovely Lucy, that police dog who always gets her man. We're sure to get nobbled."

"We won't," said Mickey. "My brain's thought everythink out."

"But how, boss? I still don't get it."

"There's not a lot you *do* get!" said Mickey. "Anyhow, I don't want to jaw about it all night. What we gonna do now is carry out a dummy-run – which ought to suit Count Dracula over there! This is what we gonna do. We're *not* going up in the lift. We gonna climb up the fire-escape – same as we'll do tomorrow. And we're gonna check everything out to make sure nothing goes wrong on the day. Okay?"

"Smart thinking, boss!" said Count Dracula. "You want to go first?"

"No," said Mickey, after a slight pause. "*You* can go first this time."

"You sure, boss? You always go first. Good job I brought my torch."

"No torches!" said Mickey. "Put it away!"

"But why, chief?" asked Minnie.

Mickey hesitated only a second. "Somebody might see us. And we do it exactly the same as tomorrow. We won't be using a torch tomorrow because it'll be broad daylight."

"Smart!" said Minnie. "You never miss a trick, chief!"

"I know," said Mickey. "Now, up the apples and pears. After you, Count Dracula, and Minnie keep close behind me. That's it, real close."

And behind his cardboard mask, Mickey firmly closed his eyes as they began to climb.

EIGHT

The Superhero

Meanwhile, Willie was still going down.

Down and down and down . . .

Four-fifths of the way down he realised his sparrots were falling – and it wasn't only his sparrots – and he cried aloud the magic words *Coconuts conquers oil* – but even that didn't do a lot of good. Five-sixths of the way down he tried waggling his hands. Six-sevenths of the way down, more in an effort to encourage himself than anything else, he said *Fly, birdy, fly!* Seven-eighths of the way down, he even squawked *Cheep! Cheep!*

But none of these brilliant ideas seemed to work.

And it occurred to Willie that perhaps, after all, a mistook had been mad.

Eight-ninths of the way down he tried again: *Mind over matter* he thought. *Simply a case of confidence. COCONUTS CONQUERS OIL!* he cried aloud.

But still it was no good.

When he was nineteen-twentieths of the way down, being a sharp lad, he began to wonder if the motto of the famous blue-blooded Obsbluds was not really *Coconuts conquers oil* but something else instead. After all, it seemed unlikely that coconuts could conquer anything. What *would* conquer things, he wondered. Of course! That was it! Courage! That was the answer. And *COURAGE CONQUERS OIL!* he screamed aloud.

And at once a message of courage, hope, valour, nobility, determination and so forth, spurted through his nobble vines until it reached every part of his spectacular body as the left leg of his dad's long-johns loomed sharply ahead. Summoning all his new-found energy he focussed his amazing intencigell on the magic words and suddenly realised he *could* fly! He really could! And that he *was* in control! He coolly pressed his palms firmly together, tipped them up (as you do at the end of a dive when you want to surface) and felt himself magically lifting upwards. And a moment later Willie alighted, a bit wobbly, on the backyard wall.

"Easy as wink!" he said to the next-door cat.

"If you ask me, it was nearly a catastrophe," said the cat, slyly.

"I didn't know cats could talk!" said Willie who, although he had long been on speaking terms with her, had never heard her speak before.

"Only when we move our lips," said the cat in a sarcastic tone of voice.

Willie rested for only a moment. Then remembering his motion in life and feeling much more confident, he took off with such a splutter of sparks that the dustbin shuddered (even though it was weighed-down with empty bean-tins and sauce bottles) as Willie shot over the ridge of the outhouses.

The cat went on polishing her whiskers.

But someone else *was* surprised. Willie's sister, burnt almost to a cinder by her latest session at the Tan-u-fast Health Studio and bedecked in gold lipstick and matching eye-shadow, was just stepping out to lighten the night-life of Muckyford, when she saw Willie spurt over the outhouse roof, trailing sparks. The sight caused her to step in again smartly.

"Our Dad," she said, "Our Willie's flying over our coalhouse."

"I just hope he's not thinking of landing on it," said Willie's dad. "There's one hole in that coalhouse roof already. We don't want no more."

"You're sure it isn't your dad's long-johns just blowing in the wind that's given you a fright, Our Darleen?" asked Mrs Scrimshaw.

"Don't think so, Our Mam. There was sparks shooting out of his boots."

"Not them new boots I've just bought him at the Co-op?" said his mam.

"I'll stop his pocket-money if he's set fire to them boots!" said his dad.

"They was green ones, Our Mam. The sparks coming out of them was red."

"Thank heavens," said Mrs Scrimshaw. "*Them's* not his Co-op boots."

"Anyroad, Our Darleen," said Mr Scrimshaw, "don't interrupt us now. It's just coming up to the right exciting bit in the Regional Quarter Finals of the All England Woofibix Left-Handed Tiddlewinks Championship!"

"Sorry, Our Dad," said Darleen, "I never knew there were something important on. But you never let *me* fly over the coalhouse roof when I were Our Willie's age!" And she pouted her beautiful golden lips.

"I don't recall as you ever wanted to, Our Darleen," said her mam. "You was always too sensible to want to fly over coalhouse roofs at his age. You was always more interested in nail varnish and pop music in them days. *And* the Royal Fambly. You get yourself to the disco, my girl, and enjoy yourself. You think you ought to go and shout him in?'' she asked her husband.

''Leave him be for a minute,'' said Mr Scrimshaw. ''Rubbish!'' he shouted as the very last left-handed tiddle was winked. ''Must want our brains examining watching a programme like that! Where's my herbal tobacco?''

''Last time I seen it you was sitting on it,'' said Mrs Scrimshaw.

''Ah, yes, here it is.'' Mr Scrimshaw filled his pipe and lit up and a smell of compost immediately filled the room. (The Kompost herbal tobacco, although it had little else to recommend it, was at least aptly named). ''It'll be all right if he's back for his chips. If he misses them chips, he can pay for them out of his pocket-money!''

''But it's not right him flying over the coalhouse, is it, Albert?''

''You can't tell none of these kids nothing nowadays!'' said Mr Scrimshaw, squiggling in his seat and distributing Kompost all round the room. ''I blame all these teachers with their new-fangled ideals! Kids watch far too much telly, if you ask me! And half of them can't speak proper. When we was at school we was always learnt to speak proper – or else!''

''Course we was,'' said Mrs Scrimshaw.

Meanwhile, far above them, Willie was flying up, up, up: far below him the cars on the motorway seemed to chug along like tiny glow-worms.

As he soared above the clouds, a couple of eider ducks flapped past him, heading north for their holidays. "You must be quackers going that way!" he joked at them. "Don't get above yourself, Scrimshaw!" they quipped back.

He went higher. Now he could see billions of stars sparkling in an endless sea of darkness. He seemed to be drawn to them, as if by a magnet. Was that where he really belonged, he wondered, up there among the stars? Was that his true home? He wondered if his real parents were missing him badly. He imagined them sitting round their radio-active fireplace, longing for a glimpse of him as they watched four-dimensional telly and were waited on hand and foot by robots. He wondered if he should go to them?

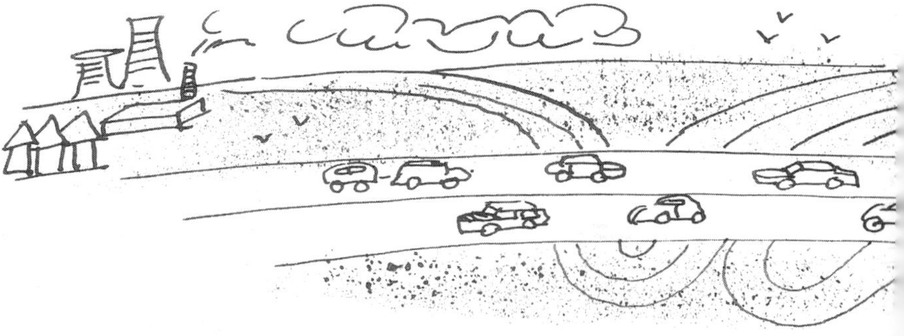

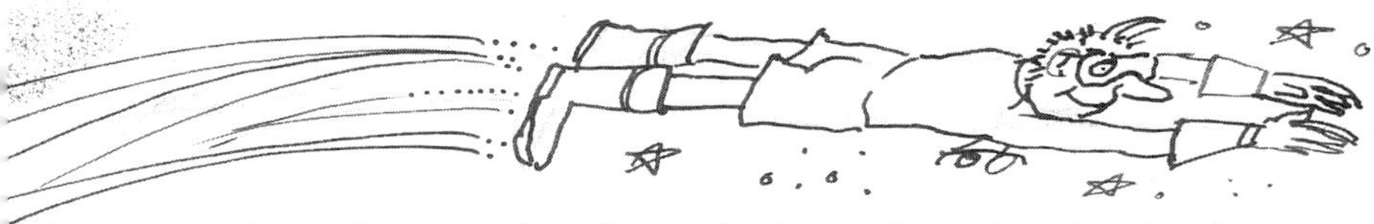

But then, as he drew in breath to begin the long journey, a familiar odour struck his nostrils: a stink of old canals and coke-works, Mr Shufflebotham's greasy chips and take-away curry so fizzing hot it burnt your brain out. A smell of lager and fag-ends, dole queues and betting-shops, his sister's horrible scent called *Pong de Paree*: the smell of Muckyford, the smell of home!

Willie turned his palms and headed downwards again until he was through the clouds and could see the familiar smelly lovely old town once more.

And with his super-powered eyes he saw something else.

A small human bean appeared to be in trouble. An angry female earthling-child was yo-yoing up and down from the bus-stop in Gasworks View like something frantic on a long piece of elastic. She was waving what appeared to be an off-white bath-towel (but he later realised was only a washed-out hanky). In the top corner of it was a stain of what – with his amazing intencigell – he recognised as his own blood! The true blue blood of The Obsbluds!

Willie Scrimshaw, superhero, gritted his almost-perfect teeth and headed on down.

NINE

To the Rescue

"Buckets of black puddens!" exclaimed Sally as Willie alighted on the pavement below her. "Where the heck did you spring from? And why are you wearing your underpants on the outside? Is that legal? You could get locked up!"

"Hail to thee, earth creature," said Willie. "I come from another planet."

"That's no excuse!" said Sally.

"I am from Outer Space," said Willie. "A superior being."

"You mean you're American?"

"Further off than that," said Willie. "I come from another galaxy. We are invincible. Our mossion is to police the universe and prevent all wrong-doing."

"You'll have a job on down here, then," said Sally. "Even the Brownies hold regular riots round our spot. What's your name?"

"If I told you my real name thou would'st not understand it," said Willie. "But," he added modestly, "if you like, you can call me Superkid."

"Now pull the other one!" said Sally, waggling her legs.

But instead of pulling her legs, Willie took the weight of them and raised her powerfully until she was unhooked, then lowered her carefully to earth.

Sally tried hard not to look impressed. "Thanks a million," she said. She looked at him under the street-lamp. "Hey up!" she said. "Don't I know you?"

"I think not, small brown-haired earthling creature," said Willie.

"Less of the *small*!" said Sally. "I'm in Miss Minsky's. Don't you go to Brick Street?" She peered up at him. "I'm sure I know those eyes and that –"

Willie narrowed his eyes. Perhaps he narrowed them so much he began to look all mean and hard because Stomper began to whimper.

"What aileth thy poor dog?" asked Willie, taking the opportunity to move into the shadow where Stomper was still tethered. "He looketh so ashamed."

(Of course he felt a twit talking like this, but what could you do when it was what folk expected?)

"He has good right to looketh so ashamed!" said Sally. "Three big lads wearing masks have just robbed me of all my money for the Endangered Animals and that daft thing should have defended me but he didn't – which is why he's an endangered animal himself now! Useless article!"

"Do not say that," said Willie. "Nobody is useless in this universe. Nothing is. Not even a spider. Not even a dead fly!"

"Urgh!" said Sally. "Do you mind!"

Willie bent down to pat Stomper. "I am sure he dideth his best – dideth you not, old feller? What's up, old chap? Did something scare you?" He untied the lead. "What is thy name?"

Stomper sniffed him. He smelled remarkably like the bony kid who lived round Balmoral Crescent. Stomper had always liked him (and not only because he resembled a bone).

"Stomper," said Stomper.

"Stomper, eh?" said Willie. "Stomper soundeth a nice name."

"What he wants," said Sally, "is a good kicketh up the backside, and how cometh you know my dog's name?"

"I have incredible powers," Willie said.

"Oh aye?" said Sally, already striding off towards Hope Street.

"Whither goest thou?" Willie called after her.

"Use your incredible powers to find out!" she shouted back. "I goeth to fetch them robbers a whump round the lughole, and get me money back!"

Willie wanted to join her in a way, but poor Stomper still looked terribly ashamed and obviously needed help.

"Feeling better now, old chap?" he said.

"No, I'm not," said Stomper. "I've let down the whole clan!"

"Clan?" said Willie. "Am I right in assuming thou hast Scottish blood?"

"Can you not see my collar?" asked Stomper, pointing at his tartan collar with a paw. "Pure-bred Scottish Terrier, I am. On both sides of the clan."

This was surprising as Stomper stood three feet at the shoulder and had black and brown spots all over (some of them in the most unfortunate places): however, Willie hid his surprise.

"Then thou wilt no doubt remember the clan motto of the Scottish Terriers?" he said. "If at first ye don't succeed, try, try, again."

"My old granny often used to say it when she was blowing on my porridge when we lived on the Isle of Dogs – ye ken that's in The Hebrides?"

"There's a lot of sense in that motto, Stomper," said Willie. "Remember it next time your sparrots begin to fall. What exactly went wrong this time?"

"I would have been all right, man, with anything but a couple of mice. But when I was a wee puppy my Uncle Hamish McKilt told me a terrible tale about mice. He once saw Mickey Mouse put a dog through a sausage machine. It came out all squidgy bits. It would not have been so bad if it had been a sausage-dog. But it was nae. Uncle Hamish said it was a big strapping handsome dog – like myself!"

Here, poor Stomper lowered his tail to half-mast.

"There, there," said Willie, patting him gently. "That's an awful tale!"

"Are you trying tae be punny?" said Stomper.

"I beggest thy pardon," said Willie. "I did not mean to embarrass thee."

"Still talking to that useless dog?" asked Sally as she came back. "Meanwhile, the robbers have vanished. We'll never find them now."

"Art thou sure?" said Willie. "Looketh at thy dog."

Stomper had his nose to the ground and was sniffing with interest.

"It was what you said, Sassenach," he said. "These things are sent to try us. Sent – scent! Get it, Sassenach? It put me in mind of my nose!" He looked round at them and tipped his head as if to say *This way, folks!*

"We could get those crooks yet!" said Sally. "Come on, Superkid!"

"Goeth thou ahead with thy dog," said Willie, "I shall try another way."

He waited until Sally and Stomper had vanished round the corner of Hope Street then launched himself into the air.

TEN

The Flying Lettuce

"Boy, what a view!" said Minnie Mouse leaning out over the rail at the top of the Observation Tower. "Come and look down here, chief!"

"No thanks, you just keep a sharp lookout," said Mickey who had his eyes tight shut and his back jammed firmly against the wall of the building behind him. He turned his head and spoke to Count Dracula off to his left. "Can you see the loudspeaker? Use your torch."

"Yeah," said Dracula, shining his torch through the window. "See it, boss?"

"Can't see a bat up here," said Mickey. "Too dark."

"Too dark?" said Minnie, turning round. "But it's like broad daylight!"

"My eyes isn't accustomed yet," said Mickey.

"Funny," said Minnie. "Can you see that plane taking off, chief?"

"Don't mention that word to me!" said Mickey.

"What word?"

"Never mind! Keep your eyes down below, where they should be! You got that door open yet?" he asked Dracula.

"Not yet, boss. Can't find the right key."

"Chief," said Minnie. "Somebody's just come through the bushes down by the pool. I think it's that little kid we left hanging around the bus-stop."

"Don't be stupid!"

"It *is* her, chief! Flipping heck! What was that?"

"What is it now?" snapped Mickey.

"Something just fizzed past under me eyes, something big!"

"Must've been a duck!" said Dracula. "I heard a couple of ducks fly past as we came up the fire escape."

"You stupid oaf!" said Mickey. "Ducks don't fly!"

"Don't they?"

"Ducks swim! Don't you know nothink?"

"Too big for a bird, anyroad," said Minnie. "Really big ugly thing!"

"Probably your nose!" said Mickey. "Where's that kid and her stupid dog?"

"Can't see them now. Maybe they've gone round to the fire-escape."

"When you gonna get this door open, idiot?"

"It *is* open, boss," said Dracula. "Can't you see?"

"Where's this loudspeaker?" asked Mickey as he blundered into the room.

"There, boss. Right in front of you. Can't you see it?"

"Perfect!" said Mickey, reaching out to feel it. "Nice big one."

"Why do we want a big loudspeaker, boss?"

"Bigger the better as far as we're concerned," said Mickey. "As long as it's joined up to the P.A. system. Which it is."

"What's a P.A. system, boss?" asked the Count.

"Public Address," explained Mickey as he took the loudspeaker from the wall and began fiddling with it. "Everybody'll hear everything said over the loudspeakers, loud and clear."

"That good, boss?"

"That's brilliant," said Mickey, making the final adjustments.

"Ch-chief?" Minnie called from outside. "Ch-chief?"

"What is it now?"

"I've just seen that big thing again. Come and see this! Qu-quick!"

"Gawd strewth!" said Dracula who had gone to the door to look out.

"What is it?" asked Mickey.

"Come and look, boss. A figure in the sky – ovvering."

"Ovvering?"

"Ovvering."

"Figures don't ovver," said Mickey.

"This one does! Come and have a look, boss! No wings or nothing."

"Don't be stupid!"

"But it's there, boss!" said Dracula. "It looks like a kid. A tough-looking kid. All dressed in green, like a flying lettuce. He's looking at us."

"He's been looking at us for five minutes now!" said Minnie.

"You pair of stupid nits!" said Mickey coming towards the door, his arms stretched out in front of him.

Then a voice rang out in the darkness. A small voice. The voice of a boy, a mere child you might say. But a voice full of authority and power, like a headmaster taking assembly or somebody invincible policing the universe.

"Might I enquire what you lotteth are up to here?" asked the voice.

Then Mickey opened his eyes. He'd never in his life seen anything so awful. The figure of a kid hanging high up in the air. And this was the awful thing: he had no visible means of support.

A giant scream escaped Mickey's lips.

A scream so loud that Sally Mow heard it halfway up the fire-escape. She had just looked down to make sure Stomper was still guarding the bottom of the steps – as she'd told him to – when the scream froze her in her tracks.

A moment later she heard the noise of three pairs of bovver boots hammering their way down the iron treads above her and knew she was done for.

There was no time to get into the shadow of the wall. She pressed herself against the guard rail and prayed they wouldn't see her in the dark.

She needn't have worried, actually. They didn't see her at all. In fact, they hardly felt her as they accidentally pushed her over the guard rail and Sally Mow began falling through the air.

She was fifty feet up when she went. The air rushed past her. Everything seemed black. Then she lost consciousness.

"What was that?" asked Dracula as they charged on down.

"What was what?" asked Minnie.

"Thought I felt something back up there, something we bumped into."

"Keep your minds on the job!" shouted Mickey, his eyes tight shut behind his mask. He opened them again as their boots hit the ground. In front of them was the stupid-looking dog they'd tied to the railings of Gasworks View.

Mickey, his eyes open again now, launched a boot at it as he passed, but I'm thankful to say he missed: Stomper was already running for his life towards the bushes, yelping with fear.

The yelps brought Sally to her senses again. She seemed to be flying through the air. No, *seemed* was the wrong word. She *was* flying. She was in the arms of the crazy-looking kid who'd rescued her down at the bus-stop.

But, of course, all that was ridiculous, wasn't it? People didn't fly. It just didn't make sense. She refused to believe it. "Do not worry, earthenchild," said Willie smiling down at her. Sally fainted again.

Willie laid her gently on the earth. He could hear the bovver boots bursting through the trees surrounding the pool and a moment later the perimeter wire shook and twanged as the thieves forced their way through the hole they'd cut, and raced down Victoria Road.

"What happened to you?" he asked Stomper who had crept out of the bushes.

"I tried my best, Sassenach!" growled Stomper.

"I'm sure thou didst," said Willie.

"It was that horrible scream that did it! I thought it was the banshees, Sassenach. Have ye heard tell of the banshees? Horrible wowling creatures that haunt the Scottish glens. I remember my mother used to tell me tales aboot them when we were having our tatie soup on the moors. I don't mind telling ye, I could have done with a drop of the hard stuff!"

"That wouldn't have done any good," said Willie. "You must stop looking at the past through tartan-coloured spectacles, Stomper. You're all bowed down under the weight of a glorious Scottish past that never existed. Throw it off your back, Stomper. Be yourself. Stand up on your own four paws and be proud of yourself, have confidence. You're Stomper. A mongrel, but a fine looking mongrel, probably born in Muckyford, where I was. But what's wrong with that?"

"What are you on about? Do you think my dear old Uncle Hamish McKilt never existed? Do you think I invented him?"

"It's possible," said Willie smiling down at him. "If he *did* exist, Stomper, he told you some pretty big fibs. Mickey Mouse never put a dog through a sausage-machine in his life. He's not that sort of a mouse at all. And while we are on about it, The Isle of Dogs isn't in the Hebrides. It's on the Thames. As for *'If at first you don't succeed, try, try again'*, that isn't an old Scottish clan motto at all. People say it all over the world, because it's good advice in any language. They probably even say it on other planets," he added wistfully, allowing himself a moment's glance at the stars.

Stomper looked at him, struck dumb for a moment.

"Talking to that dog again?" asked Sally Mow, coming awake. Beside her she saw what she at first took to be two long sticks of celery, but then realised they were probably the legs of the so-called Superkid. She scrambled to her feet. "Now I *know* you're nuts!" she said. "Nobody in their right senses talks to dogs! As for the flying bit – I just refuse to believe it. You hear me? Nobody flies. Nobody! That sort of stuff is strictly for the birds!"

"I absolutely agree," said Willie, and tucking her under one arm and Stomper under the other he flew up into the air with the pair of them.

ELEVEN

Suspicions

"You should've seen him, Willie," said Sally Mow as they walked together towards the headmaster's office next morning before registration. "Straight through the air he flew, carrying me and Our Stomper as if we were nothing. Arnold Buttermouth reckons it was an Unidentified Flying Object I saw but it definitely had legs. Come to think of it," she said, glancing down, "he had legs like yours, Willie, long skinny things. Only, his were green."

Willie smiled apologetically up at her.

"And he fair seemed to whizz through the air, Willie," she said, "like a jet-propelled salad. And while he was somehow transporting me and that daft useless dog, he said I should report everything to the headmaster. 'Get somebody to come with you,' he said. 'Somebody sensible.' "

"So you think I'm sensible, Sally?" asked Willie, hopefully.

"Do I heck!" said Sally. "You just happened to be the first article I clapped my eyes on! And you should've heard him talk, Willie. He talked that proper, a bit like Arnold Buttermouth. I *do* like folk that talk proper."

"So do I," said Willie. "When folk talk proper it's reet gradely."

"*Right* gradely," corrected Mr Watkins as he walked past them.

"And it was fair exciting when he carried me in his arms," said Sally. "I felt like one of them heroines on telly. It was like out of this world. Reckon you could carry me in *your* arms, Willie?"

"I'd have a fair good go!" said Willie.

"I reckon your knees would knock!" she said, looking again down her freckly nose, but this time more particularly at his knees, which funnily enough had won prizes in the past (though only for knobbliness). "I can't get over how he seemed to fly through the air with us," she said. "Not that folks can fly, of course, I know that. It must've been an optical illusion."

"Our Darleen can fly," said Willie.

"Don't be soft, Willie Scrimshaw!"

"She can!" said Willie. "Last year she flew from Manchester all the way to them islands off the coast of Africa that's named after some kind of birds."

"The Canary Islands, you mean?"

"No," said Willie. "The Budgies, I think they're called."

"Don't come the clever-clogs with me, Willie Scrimshaw!" she said as she made a face at him and tapped on the headmaster's door.

"With you in one moment!" called Mr Miley rousing himself from a daydream about gold-plated fifteen-day chiming clocks and his Portuguese time-share. "Enter."

"Please, Mr Miley," said Sally as they went in, "a right funny thing happened last night, which I reckon you better know about straight away."

"We haven't a lot of time this morning, Sally," said Mr Miley. "It's the big day – and from what my spies tell me you may soon be collecting Councillor Allgob's Genuine Imitation Silver-Plated Trophy for Special Effort."

"Not now, sir," said Sally. "All my money were pinched last night."

"*Was* pinched," corrected Mr Watkins as he popped in to collect his register and Miss Minsky's.

"Oh, dear! I *am* sorry to hear that!" said the headmaster. "You'd better tell me what happened. But do be quick. Mayor Allgob will be here any minute."

Sally Mow was just up to the part where she and Stomper squeezed through the hole in the fence, when Willie heard a voice outside the window of the headmaster's office, a voice that disturbed a chord in his memory.

He edged close to the window, but when he looked out, it was only a chap from the security company talking to Miss Minsky, probably about the last minute preparations down at the Swimming Complex.

Must have been mistaken, Willie thought. He was sure he'd never seen the chap's face before. But the voice sounded familiar. *Where have I heard that voice before?* he wondered. And he was trying to remember when Councillor Allgob burst into the room – which was enough to stop *any* thought.

"How do, Headmaster," he said as he came in wearing his overlong raincoat and his famous flat-hat, both dripping wet (it was always raining in Muckyford). "I'll find meself a pew." As he sat down he spilled twenty-odd sheets of paper on the floor. Willie picked them up and handed them back to him.

"Making up another of your famous speeches, Mr Allgob?" inquired Willie.

"That's right, Willie, lad. I expect you'll be looking forward to it, are you? The whole town will be, no doubt. I thought folk'd be bored stiff with all the sideshows and swimming races so I reckoned I'd just give them a bit of a treat, like, with one of my right long speeches," said the mayor.

Even listening to him for such a short time, Willie felt a huge yawn engulfing him, and by the time Sally Mow had finished explaining to the headmaster Willie had almost dozed off as the mayor droned on in his ear.

"Very interesting, Sally," said the headmaster, standing up. "Ingenious idea, that some kind of robbery is going to take place. To be honest, the security firm haven't told me their plans. I *do* happen to know they transported Miss Minsky's school desk to somewhere secret yesterday, but it's hardly likely they've taken it to the top floor of the Observation Tower, is it? The top floor of the Observation Tower is surely the *last* place you'd expect them to keep the money. In any case, Lovely Lucy and her three handlers are personally helping to guard the money, so I'm sure you'll find everything is fine! I'm afraid you've let your imagination run away with you this time, Sally Mow. Not like you!"

"My old dad used to say imagination were a very fine thing, but it don't score no goals," said the mayor. "Or were it butter no turnips?"

"But the point is, Mr Mayor-" started Willie, politely.

"Run along now, Willie," said Mr Miley gently as he shooed them out.

"Another of my dad's sayings were -" started the mayor.

But fortunately for Willie and Sally, at that moment the headmaster charitably closed the door behind them.

TWELVE

Zzzzzz

As usual Miss Minsky made her class walk down to the Complex boys and girls separately, but at least when they got down there everything seemed okay.

Willie and Sally had a look round the back of the Observation Tower and were glad to see a patrol car parked there, with three beefy policemen in it and the Lovely Lucy as well.

The parents flooded in from all the surrounding streets and spent money like water at the side-shows because they knew it was a good cause. And when the races began, Willie managed to get the seat next to Sally Mow, the only snag being that there was a nail sticking up on it (though, at the time, that didn't seem important).

As he sat down there were only three things worrying Willie:

First, Arnold Buttermouth had sat himself on the other side of Sally and was gabbing away at her so much that Willie could hardly get a word in edgeways.

Secondly, he saw the security guard lugging away a sack of money and, when he called out something, Willie felt absolutely positive he'd heard the chap's voice before. But where?

Thirdly, something the headmaster had said kept niggling at his mind. *The top floor of the Observation Block is surely the last place you'd expect them to keep the money.* There seemed nothing wrong with that sentence. It seemed perfectly sensible. And yet . . .

"THANK YOU FOR YOUR GENEROSITY, LADIES AND GENTLEMEN, BOYS AND GIRLS," said Mr Watkins over the P.A. system. He was sitting at a table in front of the stands, wearing a straw hat and his tie almost undone – obviously trying to look like a pop star. "OUR RACES WILL BEGIN IN A MOMENT WHILE OUR CAPABLE MISS MINSKY ADDS UP THE TAKINGS SO FAR." Here he blushed slightly and lifted his eyes to heaven. Did he think she was an angel or something? Willie wondered. "REMEMBER, IF YOU HAVE NOT ALREADY DONE SO YOU CAN SPONSOR ANY SWIMMER OR DIVER AT ANY TIME. THE GIRL OR BOY RAISING THE MOST MONEY WILL RECEIVE THE COUNCILLOR ALLGOB GENUINE IMITATION SILVER-PLATED

TROPHY FOR SPECIAL EFFORT, KINDLY DONATED BY COUNCILLOR ALLGOB AND HIS GOOD LADY WIFE."

Everybody clapped.

The mayor glanced up from his notes. His good lady wife – who for some reason was wearing her double-knit woolly hat – smiled graciously.

"LATER ON, WHEN MISS MINSKY UP THERE," said Mr Watkins, blushing again, "HAS MADE THE FINAL COUNT, COUNCILLOR ALLGOB WILL KINDLY GIVE US A SPEECH."

Some cheeky people began to boo and shout, "Mercy! Mercy!"

But Willie hardly heard them. *Up there?* he was thinking. Had Mr Watkins really said that? He glanced up at the top of the Observation Tower. Was it possible that Miss Minsky really was up there?

The swimming races had started now. Just before each one there was a rush to add sponsor money at the desks positioned round the pool, and a few minutes after each event there was a further announcement, such as: "LADIES AND GENTLEMEN, WE ARE HAPPY TO ANNOUNCE A NEW LEADER IN THE RACE FOR THE COUNCILLOR ALLGOB GENUINE IMITATION SILVER-PLATED TROPHY FOR SPECIAL EFFORT. LIONEL RAMSBOTHAM, WINNER OF THE BACKSTROKE, HAS JUST RAISED NINE POUNDS!"

Now it was the high diving. Shrimp was up there in his silver shorts, ready for his final dive. He looked so calm. So perfect. So like a sardine.

Willie remembered how *he'd* felt up there: scared to death. Yet last night, as he zoomed up over the coalhouse he'd felt as if cut-free from dragging chains that usually bound him to earth. And as he had zoomed higher and higher – above the high-board, above the clouds – he hadn't felt the slightest tremor of fear. Quite the reverse. But he knew that the kid who flew through the air without fear was exactly the same one who the day before had been shaking like a jelly on the high board. How could that be? Had The Messenger been right when he told him it was just a case of mind over matter? Did it all depend on the way you thought about yourself? On confidence? Could courage *really* conquer oil? Come to think of it, even *that* didn't sound right now.

"Great, isn't it, eh not?" said Sally Mow, digging him in the ribs.

"Eh?" said Willie, looking up at the top board, expecting to see Shrimp Salmon. But no Shrimp Salmon was there. He had gone. And now five swimmers were poised on the starting blocks at one end of the pool.

"What happened?" asked Willie. "Did Shrimp win?"

"Course he did, you cloth-head!" said Sally. He's collected nine pounds and ninety pence in sponsor money with that dive. He's just taken the lead! Didn't you hear the announcement? I expect you were dreaming again, Willie Scrimshaw! You're like

I-don't-know-what! Now it's the last race. Can you see Arnold?"

Willie couldn't. He could see five swimmers getting ready to go. But no Arnold.

"Where is he?" asked Willie.

"Halfway up the pool," said Sally.

Willie could see him now. "But why?" he asked.

"His mam says his cold's got worse, so he has half a length start this time, instead of ten yards. Just to give him a chance."

"I didn't know his cold was worse," said Willie.

Sally just gave him one of her looks.

It was an exciting race. Most girls were screaming for Arnold as the other five swimmers gained on him all the way. In the end it looked like two had overtaken him, but Mrs Buttermouth, who was chief judge, said Arnold had won by a whisker. Three girls swooned in the long grass, and that was that.

"ARNOLD BUTTERMOUTH IS THE WINNER OF THE FINAL EVENT, LADIES AND GENTLEMEN," said Mr Watkins, "AND ACCORDING TO MISS MINSKY'S CALCULATIONS" – here he blushed again – "HE IS ALSO THE WINNER OF THE COUNCILLOR ALLGOB GENUINE IMITATION SILVER-PLATED TROPHY, WITH A FINAL TOTAL OF TEN POUNDS EXACTLY! GIVE HIM A BIG HAND, FOLKS!"

They all gave him a big hand, but Willie couldn't help thinking what a shame it was that Sally hadn't won. If she hadn't had her money nicked she'd have won it by a penny (*his* penny).

But now somebody must have stuck a pin in the headmaster because he was on his feet, and almost awake. "And now I call on Councillor Allgob to present the prizes," he said, before collapsing in his seat and nodding off again.

"MY DEAR OBJECTS AND CONSTITUENT PARTS," said the mayor as he got to his feet, and his lady wife smiled graciously and pulled her double-knit hat solidly down over her earholes, "UNACCUSTOMED AS I AM TO PUBLIC SPEAKING, IT GIVES ME GREAT PLEASURE TO BE ALLOWED TO ADDRESS YOU FOR THE NEXT TWO HOURS OR SO. AS MY DEAR OLD DAD USED TO SAY..."

Everybody groaned.

Willie took a big breath and yawned (with his hand over his mouth).

"I WELL REMEMBER THE DAY IN 1932," Councillor Allgob was saying, and it seemed to Willie that the mayor's words were getting louder every second. Willie stifled another yawn. He noticed that Sally Mow had put on her ear-muffs. She gave him a cheeky sideways smile. He wouldn't have minded ear-muffs himself. They might have shut out the noise of Councillor Allgob.

She wasn't the only one to have thought of that wheeze Willie noticed. The security guard, whose voice he thought he'd recognised, was taking away the last sackful of sponsor money and *he* had headphones on now. And that again stirred a chord in

Willie's memory. Who else had told him something about headphones? Who was it? Somebody. And was he barmy or was the mayor's speech getting even louder? And louder? And louder . . . Or was that just a dream?

THIRTEEN

Sally Alone

On and on and on droned the mayor's speech. It was an Allgob Special.

Willie could see people falling asleep all round him. Arnold Buttermouth had returned to his seat and his wobbly chin had already sunk on to his chest. Even Mr Watkins was looking decidedly dreamy. Willie, too, wanted to sleep. It was like being in a double Maths lesson. But he knew he had to stay awake.

He knew there was something highly significant about that security guard wearing headphones: but what the significant fact was, he hadn't a clue.

He had an idea that somebody, somewhere, had told him something about headphones, but trying to think who it was or where or why it was, with the mayor droning on, was like trying to walk on a sea of feathers or was it cotton wool or was it clouds or was it -

"Up there!" said Sally's voice in his ear. "Look up there, Willie!"

Why did she want him to look up there at the diving-board? he wondered. Was Shrimp Salmon about to dive? No, of course not! He remembered that Shrimp had already dived. And he remembered something else: Shrimp's story about three big lads listening to silence. Why should anyone listen to silence? It didn't make sense. The only thing he could think of – and that was a joke – was that listening to silence would be a lot better than listening to Councillor Allgob. But it was no time for jokes of course.

An elbow jabbed in his ribs. "Not at the diving-board, Willie! Up there!"

Up there? Willie wondered. Did she mean behind him?

He scrunched himself round and looked back up into the grandstand. The mayor was still going strong. Everybody else had allowed their eyes to glaze over, as if in a long assembly. His mam and dad were snoring in unison, his sister Darleen was making fluttery noises through her golden lips. Even the starlings in the rafters were dropping off to sleep!

Willie's own eyes were dying to be closed. Aching to be. He needed something to prop them open. Matchsticks might do.

"Open your eyes, lummock! Look up there!"

The elbow went into his ribs again. He realised that Sally seemed to be pointing at the top of the Observation Tower. But why? Something had happened at the top of the Observation Tower, he knew that, he could remember that. Something important.

But what was it?

And then a brilliant idea struck him. He knew now what was funny about the headmaster's words. Of course! The last place you'd expect a security company to keep money would be the very place they *would* keep it! But that was crazy, wasn't it? Miss Minsky always said he was dreaming. Dreaming . . .

"Willie! Lughead! Cod lump!"

Even these loving words failed to rouse him.

For the third time he felt her sharp elbow and he struggled awake for a moment, but it was hard keeping his eyes open for even a fraction of a second. In a moment of perfect clarity he realised it was silly thinking of matchsticks at a moment like this: it was pit-props he needed now. It wasn't pit-props he needed, actually. It was telegraph poles. Even telegraph poles would crack and give way under the strain.

"Willie? Can you hear me? I'm going now."

He forced his eyes open. A damsel in distress . . . "FURTHERMORE, the mayor was saying, IN THE BROAD GENERAL PRINCIPLE OF EXTENDING THE AVAILABILITY OF PUBLIC FACILITIES . . ." His voice seemed even louder now. It seemed to fill the entire grandstand, the entire Swimming Complex now, the whole of Muckyford. It seemed to be filling his head.

"Willie! Willie! Why did you just say 'telegraph poles'?"

But Willie didn't answer.

"I need your help, Willie Scrimshaw! Do you hear me? I'm asking you to help me! Are you coming or not? Willie!" She shook him. But it was no use. He was fast asleep. Maybe Miss Minsky was right, she thought, and all men were useless when you needed them most. In that case, she thought, she'd have to manage without them, like her mam had done all these years.

She started across the grass. She knew what was going on now, and that somebody had to warn the police. *Nobody makes a monkey out of me!* she thought.

She passed Mr Watkins, fast asleep at his desk, his straw hat fallen off to reveal a small bald patch at the top of his napper, and she realised with a shock he must be quite old really, probably nearly thirty.

When she reached the Observation Tower she turned and looked back to see if silly Willie Scrimshaw was galloping to her aid like some nutty knight in one of his own daft stories, but to her great disappointment he wasn't.

She turned the corner and saw Stomper standing there. He seemed to be trying to tell her something, but of course she hadn't time to waste on silly dogs now. She ordered him to go home, but the stupid animal didn't seem to understand. She saw that Lovely Lucy and her policemen were no longer in their car, and that gave her some hope. Maybe they were already making an arrest. She went to the lift.

She pressed the button once, twice and again. But it seemed to be stuck, halfway up the tower as far as she could see.

She started up the fire-escape, glad now she hadn't sold her last pair of ear-muffs, because at least they would enable her to stay awake and assist Lovely Lucy and the police to save the charity money.

But when she turned the corner at the top it wasn't the police and Lovely Lucy she saw: it was Mickey Mouse, Minnie Mouse and Count Dracula. And in half a tick they'd bound and gagged her and thrown her in the room where Miss Minsky was tied to her desk: smart, elegant and fast asleep.

FOURTEEN

Willie Gets the Point

Willie was floating feet first down a long river between banks thick with masses of the famous flat-hat plant and the overlong raincoat trees.

Only one thing threatened to disturb his slumber.

Something with sharp teeth kept nibbling his ankle. At first he thought it was a crocodile, but then he realised it couldn't be a crocodile because crocodiles didn't nibble your ankle, they swiped your whole leg off instead. Then he thought it might be Sally Mow's elbow, but realised it couldn't be that either, because elbows didn't have teeth. Sharp thinking, Scrimshaw! he thought.

Unfortunately, smart thinking didn't stop the nibbling – and an extra-special nibble woke him with a start and he saw – of all things – Stomper.

"What are you doing here?" he asked sleepily.

Of course, Stomper replied at once, but Willie couldn't understand a word, partly because the mayor's words were even louder now, and partly because Willie wasn't wearing his magic suit. But when he noticed that the seat next to him was empty and he saw the worried look in Stomper's eyes he realised that Sally was in some kind of danger and that brought him quickly to his senses.

Fighting against sleep, he unzipped his sports bag, turned it inside-out, and began to dress, and almost at once he understood Stomper's words:

"So like I say, buster," he was saying, "I just thought I'd mosey over and have a look at Lovely Lucy. Some doll! And I was just giving her the eye-"

"Excuse me," said Willie, "but why are you talking American now?"

"Didn't I explain, buddy boy?" said Stomper. "I was thinking over what you said about this Scottish stuff. And you was right! All baloney! Then I remembered my mother was born in Hollywood. Why are you looking at me like that? She was an old-time movie queen. I was just telling Lovely Lucy all about it. Boy! Is she one captivating canine? And she seemed real interested."

"Stomper," said Willie patiently, yanking on his left boot, "this is no time for romance. Pray sticketh to the facts."

"Well," said Stomper, "even as I was chatting her up she and her assistants got a call for help from the top of the Observation Tower and they rushed to the lift."

"And?" said Willie, drawing on a gauntlet.

"They got stuck. About halfway up."

"I begin to see all now," said Willie. "Thy mistress is in direst danger."

"Don't I know it!" said Stomper. "I tried to warn her, but you know what human beings are like. We always call them dumb animals. She started up the fire-escape and ordered me home, but I knew I was needed, so I came for you."

''But how didst thou knowest I was here?'' Willie asked.

''Instinct,'' said Stomper. ''Let's move it, buddy boy. On my way here I heard her screaming for help.''

''Ow!'' said Willie as he shuffled back to adjust his underpants.

''What is it?'' asked Stomper.

''Nothing. I think I just sat on a small nail.''

''This is no time for minor points, Buster,'' said Stomper. ''The point is, three females need our help. You know who's got them? I saw them looking down at me from the tower. Mickey Mouse, Minnie Mouse and their batty friend!''

''And thou art not afraid, Stomper?''

''Afraid? I'm terrified. But a dog's gotta do what a dog's gotta do.''

''Attaboy, Stomper!'' said Willie. ''You go to the foot of the fire-escape, and this time you let no one pass, you hear me? Not like last night!''

''Hot diggety! I haven't a clue what you're on about, buster!'' said Stomper, screwing up his face and stomping off.

Then Willie lifted his lean, powerful arms above his head, concentrated hard and began to fly through the air.

But not quite in the way he expected.

FIFTEEN

'Courage Conquers Oil'

Have you ever blown up a balloon and then let it go without tying it properly?

That's more or less what happened to Willie.

He rose two feet in the air and circled jerkily through the grandstand, all the time emitting a disgusting *wwwhhhrrrupppp!* sound. Then he collapsed in a heap only a few yards away from where he'd started. On his second attempt he did a lot better, and almost clonked his napper on the high board before executing a perfect crash-landing in the foot-bath.

"Stop showing off!" Stomper called back to him.

Willie gritted his near-perfect teeth. Something was wrong, he knew. The old magic didn't seem to be there, his strength was draining away from him.

But he knew something else: Sally Mow was in danger.

So once more he hurled himself skywards.

This time he managed to land halfway up the fire-escape. Looking down he could see Stomper, looking suitably determined and grim. He seemed to have his mind on the job. (In fact, Stomper was thinking of a cartoon he'd seen last night on television. But Willie didn't know that.) And even though Willie was exhausted by his latest efforts, it cheered him to think he had one ally.

Once more Brave Sir William charged into battle, he told himself, then he began to climb. The iron rungs of the fire-escape shook beneath him, reflecting the shakiness within his feet which grew with every step. He began to mutter, *Mind over matter! Mind over matter! Confidence!* Nearing the top he recited loudly the names of his illustrated forefathers: Cousin Bravvoguts Slobsgod; Grandad Neagle who, never forget, held the banner at the Battle of Borts; Sickbert of the Flashing Blade; and not forgetting his nobble Father.

Then, as he turned the final corner and saw his enemies, he cried aloud the gallant motto of the Obsbluds, *Courage conquers oil!,* and flung himself into the fray.

SIXTEEN

An Awkward Spot

But I'm afraid it didn't do him a lot of good.

As he turned the corner, Willie had the look of a lettuce three weeks past its sell-by date, and in no time at all he was overpowered, flung into the small room and the iron door locked behind him.

He saw Miss Minsky bound to her school desk, fast asleep, and Sally Mow tied to a small chair, still wide awake. Willie dragged his weary limbs over to the loudspeaker and with one mighty wrench almost tore away the wiring. With the second he succeeded, and a blessed silence filled the room.

"Thou can taketh off thy ear-muffs now, earth-child," Willie said as he unbound Sally Mow. Then he started to untie Miss Minsky.

"Heavens!" said Miss Minsky, starting awake. "I've just had the most awful nightmare. I dreamed I was chained to that desk for the rest of my life. Who on earth are you?"

"A superior being," said Willie, modestly.

"Men!" said Miss Minsky. She clicked her tongue and turned her head away.

"If you're *that* blinking superior," said Sally, "how come you're stuck in here with us?"

"I did my best," said Willie apologetically to Sally.

"Is that what you call it? There's blood dripping down your nose," said Sally. "You look like you've walked through a wall. Come here and I'll dab it off for you. There's no need to look so sheepish. One little drop of blood and you men are frightened to death." She took out a hanky – another faded, well-washed one, as it happened – and began to dab at the trickle of blood. But in doing so she must have come dangerously close to Willie's nose because she sprang back shouting, "I know that nose! I know I know that nose!"

"I know that nose as well," said Miss Minsky, going pale at the memory. "If I'm not mistaken I've often seen it standing by this very desk waiting to get its sums marked!"

"Verily, earth-maidens, thou must be mistaken!" said Willie, hurriedly taking the handkerchief from Sally and covering the lower half of his face while pretending to dab at the blood. "I was born of a warrior race far –"

"Huh!" said Miss Minsky.

"You're right, miss," said Sally. Then turning to Willie she asked: "If you're a warrior, how come you got beaten up? Didn't you tell me last night you were invincible?"

"I should have said *practically* invincible," said Willie. "According to the rules I should have been able to beat those three thugs out there. But for some reason my powers seemed to fade."

"I've heard that one before and all!" said Miss Minsky.

"Mind, miss," said Sally, "he *was* pretty nifty

last night. He flew through the air with the greatest of ease with me and Stomper under his arms."

"If you say so," said Miss Minsky, "though one could hardly believe it, looking at the creature now."

"He fair took my breath away last night," Sally said. She turned back to Willie. "Has summat happened to you since?"

"Nothing," said Willie. "Except . . ."

He was about to mention the rip in his costume but stopped. He remembered just in time that the rip had occurred in an area that no gentleman would mention in the presence of a lady.

"Spit it out!" said Sally. "We weren't born yesterday."

Shyly, Willie explained about the rip in his magic suit, and its precise location. "I suspect that's why my powers have faded," he said. "There is a high-tech repair outfit beneath my left armpit, shouldst thou find it of use."

"Give it here, daft noodle!" Sally said. Willie reached under his left armpit and handed her a small plastic wallet. "Is this what you call high-tech?" she said. "It's nowt but a needle and thread!"

As Sally threaded the needle, Miss Minsky – whose considered opinion was that all women should be either barristers or brain surgeons – said sniffily: "Can't this so-called invincible person even do his own darning?"

"It *is* in a bit of an awkward spot, like, miss," said Sally. "Bend over!"

Willie felt depressed as he bent over. Just beyond the solid door he could hear the thieves laughing. He'd never felt so useless in his life.

"It's probably all a waste of time!" he said. "I fear it will do no good."

"Faint heart never won fair–" started Sally, but she stopped herself just in time and began to sew.

Miss Minsky said nothing, but just looked disappointed in Sally.

Beyond the door they could hear Mickey joking as he lugged the last of the sacks to the top of the fire-escape. If he'd looked over the parapet and inspected the scene below, which he didn't (Mickey kept his eyes tight shut behind the mask and you've probably guessed the reason for *that*) he would have seen how perfectly his plans had worked out.

Councillor Allgob looked good for another three hours. He had just finished his first interesting point

– on the new bogs in Burke Street – and was about to pass on to the valuable work done by his nephew Bollinger Allgob, on the Sub-committee For the Provision of Bin Bags. Meanwhile his audience, which by now included most of Muckyford, slept on obliviously.

Spodger smiled. Soon they'd have all the loot down the fire-escape and into the patrol-car. Then he was going to persuade the other two idiots to stay behind while he drove off to catch a fast boat to Spain (not a plane, of course, and you've probably guessed the reason for that and all) for the perfect life, drinking lager on the Costa Brava, forever.

But that last, heaviest sackful made a terrible dragging sound which reached beyond the iron door and into the heart of Willie Scrimshaw, who was still bent over forwards in an embarrassing position. He sprang up with a cry of "Oh!"

"Sorry," said Sally. "Did I jab you with my needle?"

"No," said Willie. "It's just that I must stop those villains!"

"I haven't quite finished yet," said Sally.

"Stand back, earth-maidens!" commanded Willie, who was feeling fizzier already. "I have work to do!" And turning to the door he cried aloud, "Courage conquers oil!"

"I beg your pardon?" said Miss Minsky.

"Courage conquers oil," Willie explained, "is the motto of us Obsbluds."

"You silly boy!" said Miss Minsky. "You mean '*we* Obsbluds,' not 'us'. And you don't mean 'Courage conquers oil', you mean 'Courage conquers *all!*' "

Willie looked at her blankly for a moment. Perhaps she was right. Teachers *were* supposed to know everything. He turned once more to the door.

"COURAGE CONQUERS ALL!" he shouted.

Miss Minsky uttered a squeak and fell back in her chair. Sally went white. Even Willie was somewhat taken-aback.

For the iron door had burst from its hinges.

SEVENTEEN

A Stuff Called Courage

What followed was never properly described by Mickey, Minnie and the Count. In all the years that followed not one of them uttered a word on the subject.

So the only reliable witnesses we have are Miss Minsky and Sally Mow.

Miss Minsky never did say much on the subject, but she was a different woman afterwards.

Sally Mow *did* speak out. In great detail. And when we listen to what she says, we must remember that being the sort of girl who got high marks for needlework and who generally thought 'poetry were junk', she would normally have been regarded as a most reliable witness; which is what makes her description all the more remarkable.

For a start off, it was full of oldy-worldy words and phrases like *gallant, hero, light of courage seemed to blaze in his eyes* etc. Exactly the sort of high-flown rhubarb that's always popping up in poems.

Then there are the claims she made for Superkid. For a start, she says that his first move was to dive upwards – whoever heard of anybody diving *upwards*? Then she says that as he descended there were blue sparks coming out of his ears. Absolute rubbish, of course. And, finally, she says that he tied Count Dracula in a knot, when in fact no fewer than fourteen international experts have testified that this was quite impossible and that a freak wind at the top of the Observation Tower must have caused this phenomenon.

I'm afraid it seems that Count Dracula put up very little of a fight. A *WAZONK* and two *KERPOYS* and he was already planning to keep Muckyford tidy for the rest of his life.

Minnie Mouse lasted a little longer: three seconds. He required not only a *WAZONK* and two *KERPOYS* but also a *YAMMERSLAMMER* before he went down on his knees and begged Willie to spare his life so he could start his Seven Days A Week Youth Club for all the little kids in the area.

Spodger Bodger was a different matter. Spodger was not just an ugly mug, a shaven head, and fourteen revolting tattoos. It was not for nothing that he wore a badge in his cowboy hat that said Marshall Harts. He fought long and hard. Again and again he swatted Willie down. But Willie kept getting up and getting up (you will no doubt remember that Willie was pretty good at this).

A magic suit is okay, of course. And a body that's muscles all over can come in handy. But neither of these is the least bit of good if you haven't got something else. All sorts of folk have this other stuff. You don't have to be brainy to have it, or daft, or weak, or strong, or short, or long. Boxers can have it, so can librarians. You can have it when you're seventy or seven. You can have it if you're pink, white, black or green. You can't buy it in a shop and you'll never find it free in the bottom of a cornflake packet.

It's a stuff called courage, and though a lot of people imagine they've never had it, one day they'll find it buried deep inside them.

And the courage of the Obsbluds spurted through Willie's vines now as he fought and fought, reciting the whole while under his breath the illustrated names of his Cousin Bravvoguts Slobsgod; Grandad Neagle who, never forget, held the banner at The Battle of Borts; Sickbert of the Flashing Blade; and not forgetting his Nobble Father.

And yet, for all this, Willie was losing.

It was true Spodger was tiring, but Willie was tiring faster. His strength and power were draining away (I know I need hardly explain to you why) and there came a time when he could rise no more and could only watch helplessly as Spodger Bodger, thankful the battle was over, grabbed the loot and began to descend down the fire-escape with nothing on this earth left to stop him.

EIGHTEEN

Snappy Pants

Now when I say *nothing* I tell a slight lie.

Two chapters back you probably thought how irresponsible it was of Stomper to be thinking of a cartoon while he stood guard at the bottom of the fire-escape.

But there you would have been wrong.

In the cartoon, a bulldog called Blitzy had twice failed his master by running away from a burglar, but at the very end had redeemed his good name by seizing the burglar (also at the very end). And, as so often happens, Stomper had seen his own serious problems perfectly reflected in this silly cartoon and had decided to act accordingly.

It was true that Stomper and Blitzy did not look exactly alike. Blitzy had bigger shoulders, bigger teeth, a bigger chest, and a truly revolting profile. But apart from that, the two were identical.

So when Stomper heard the fire-escape rocking under the weight of Spodger Bodger, he practised his very best growl, gritted his teeth and tried to make his ears sizzle, the way Blitzy's had done.

And he stayed like that until Spodger came into view wearing his mask – and the moment he saw that mask Stomper went a very limp shade of pale inside and his sinews turned to soft putty.

"What's up, Superkid?" Sally Mow was asking six flights up.

Willie didn't reply. To be honest, he hadn't the strength.

Besides, he felt ashamed because he'd let down all his famous forbears.

And there was something else he felt ashamed of.

"*I* know what's up!" said Sally, "and *you* do as well! Didn't I say we ought to finish the job properly? But *you* wouldn't listen! Too busy galloping off on your high horse saving the universe. Bend over, Snappy-pants!"

"I beggest thy pardon?" said Willie.

"I said bend over, Snappy-pants!" said Sally. "Let's get this job properly finished." She flourished the needle. "We'll have you right in two shakes of a lamb's tail. I'm sharper than you think."

"Ow!" said Willie.

"Awfully sorry!" said Sally, "but I have work to do!"

Now when Stomper's sinews turned soft and his insides went pale you probably thought, *Oh-oh! This dratted dog is going to chicken out again!*

But you would have been wrong once more.

It is true that when he saw Mickey Mouse

coming towards him, he *felt* like chickening out. It's true he had a strong desire to duck his responsibilities, that he felt cold turkey. Yes, I even admit that his heart began to quail.

But then he remembered that Blitzy, too, had been anxious when he was confronted for the third time by the burglar – just before he shoved aside his cowardly fears and waded in like a proper bulldog oughta.

Which was what Stomper did now. Gnashers gnashing, teeth flashing, paws pawing. A terrible sight.

Not that Spodger was scared. He came on, growling like a dog himself, boots and fists flying in all directions.

And I expect you thought that hurt Stomper?

Well, there you would have been right.

A lot of Spodger's kicks and blows landed, and Stomper's ears certainly began to sizzle, though not quite in the way Stomper had hoped.

But Stomper held on.

To be precise, it took Sally Mow less than a couple of ticks to mend the magic suit, but to poor Stomper six flights below it felt like a very long time, and every hour getting tougher. It was just as his right ear finally sizzled off in the direction of the perimeter fence, that Willie arrived – like a green thunderbolt out of the blue.

What followed was, of course, unseen by human eye apart from Willie himself (who was too modest to say anything), and Spodger Bodger who never spoke out on the subject (but who immediately after set up The Spodger Bodger Home for Lost Little Kittens).

There was a *WHAM!* a *SLAMBANG!* a *POWEE!* three *KERUNCHES!* and a *BOING!* and it was all over for Spodger Bodger.

When Sally Mow turned the last corner on her way down the fire-escape she was just in time to see Spodger on his knees to Superkid saying:

"I seen the light! I seen the light!"

It wasn't grammar of course and Mr Watkins would have fainted on the spot. But under the circumstances it would have to do. And Willie dealt out no more *SLAMS, POWEES,* or *KERUNCHES* or BOINGS. Instead, he directed his X-ray eyes to look at the down-button of the lift. At once the lift began to descend. Then he turned to Spodger and said: "There is one more lesson thou must learn."

"What's going on?" asked Sally.

"Take my other hand," Willie said to her. "Fasten your safety-belts!"

Then silently, powerfully, effortlessly, he rose into the air with the pair of them (not to mention the money-bags) as if they were no more substantial than figments of his imagination.

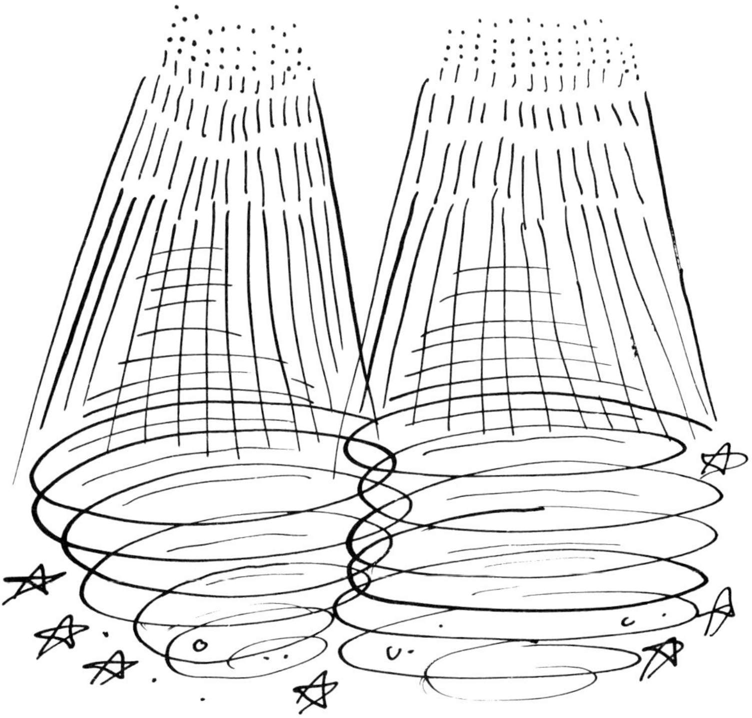

NINETEEN

High Flyers

As they circled above the swimming pool, something unheard-of happened. Councillor Allgob stopped speaking! Catching sight of three people and several money-bags flying towards the top diving board his well-developed jaw began to fall and his mouth formed a very large, and delightfully silent, O.

The sudden rush of silence awoke the crowd who – when they saw Willie and his passengers curvetting through the air – uttered a loud admiring AAAAAAAHHH! that filled the grandstand. Then they watched breathlessly as Willie alighted on the top diving board and set Sally carefully down behind him.

"Thou art not afraid, oh small and earthenware creature?" he enquired.

"Don't be potty!" said Sally, though to be honest she was feeling the teeniest bit wobbly (but she wasn't going to admit that, especially to a boy).

As for poor Spodger, Willie had set him down at the far end of the board and he was grovelling on his hands and knees, trying to cling on with all fours.

"P-please let me d-down," he kept saying. "I want to start my h-home for p-pussy cats!"

"A most noble ambition, varlet," said Willie, "but first thou must return this young damsel's money."

"I haven't touched a penny of it," Spodger said, handing it over.

"We are glad to hear it," said Willie. "And, now, oh skinheaded and mightily-tattooed one, how strong art thy braces?"

"P-pretty strong," said Spodger through ch-chattering teeth.

"In that case they should support you ever more!" said Willie, slyly. He reached out and in half a tick Spodger was hanging from the diving board suspended only by the strength of his own braces.

"P-please don't leave me here!" shouted Bodger as he bounced up and down like a baby in its bouncer.

"The sooner thou confesseth all, the sooner thou wilt get down," said Willie. "I shall then send somebody up to rescue thee. Farewell!"

And so saying, he seized Sally's hand firmly in his and sailed down with her to the front of the grandstand where he landed perfectly, just as Miss Minsky staggered towards them.

"That young man has just saved all the charity money!" she gasped. "I saw him singlehandedly defeat three husky criminals! He was *magnificent!*" she said. "He has opened my eyes to the beauties of nature," she added, glancing sideways at Mr Watkins. "He is a true hero!" Then she collapsed into Mr Watkins's arms – which happened to be conveniently near by.

A lot of applause and clapping broke out for

Willie, but naturally he waved it aside. "My Lord Mayor, Lady Mayoress, teachers, Ordinary Earthlings," he said when all were silent, "know ye, that I come from afar, from another planet in fact."

"OOOOOOOOH!" said everybody.

"Beautiful grammar!" exclaimed Mr Watkins. "Say on, oh creature from afar!"

"Know ye, that our purpose is to pacify Earth."

"EEEEEEEEH!"

"And that today," said Willie, "I have rescued the money from yon varlet up yonder!" Here he pointed backwards with a rather theatrical gesture (picked up, I'm afraid, from a pantomime his Aunty Flora had taken him to see at the Muckyford Alhambra) and with a cry of "Lo and behold" threw down the sacks of money on to the floor!

"OOOOH HECK!" said everybody.

"So ye might say," said Willie.

"Marvellous phraseology!" said Mr Watkins. "Could I possibly have your autograph after the speech?"

"I'm afraid not," said Willie, though not without a touch of regret. "Soon I must depart for other missions. But first," said Willie, looking around rather innocently, "is there by any chance a headmaster in the grandstand?"

"Finally," said Mr Miley, standing up and almost waking up, "I would like to thank you most sincerely for the gold plated twenty-one day Portuguese clock which I shall always treasure in my chiming time-share -" He broke off when he caught sight of Willie. "Good gracious me! Is that a giant salad I see before me? Is it time for lunch already? I thought it was Thursday. Where are my specs?"

"You have them on, Headmaster," said Mr Watkins, not unkindly.

"Headmaster," said Willie, with a slight, but respectful nod of the head, "I think Miss Minsky will find this young woman has collected ten pounds and one penny for the Endangered Animal fund –" here he handed over the money to Miss Minsky – "and that she has therefore won the Prize for Special Effort."

"Correct!" declared Miss Minsky, adding up the contents at a glance.

"In that case, young woman," said the mayor, "I have much pleasure in awarding you my Genuine Imitation Silver-Plated Trophy for Special Effort!"

Sally had blushed when Willie had referred to her as a young woman, but now, as she accepted the trophy and the whole school clapped and cheered, she blushed even more.

"What about a consolation prize for my poor little Arnold?" said Mrs Buttermouth, slipping a box of chocolates to the mayor. "They can be paid for out of the School Fund, later. Poor lad's blubbing his eyes out."

"Good idea," said the mayor. "Poor lad!" And he handed over the chocolates to Arnold saying "To a very gallant loser!" aloud, and more quietly to Arnold, "Thank your dad, lad, for the very nice cheque he sent for my Special Amenities Fund and tell him I am personally highly delightipated!"

Arnold nodded, winked, sniffed and wiped a tear from his eye with his hanky as he accepted the chocolates.

"And to resume my speech," said the mayor, "as my old dad used to say -"

"Shut up and sit down, Albert!" said the mayor's lady wife.

"Thank you, madam," said Willie. "I am sure we are all grateful for that. Before I depart I would also like to mention that without this young woman's aid – I believe her name is Sally Mow – my efforts would have been as naught."

A further cheer broke out in the crowd and Sally blushed even more.

"Furthermore," said Willie, after allowing the cheers to die down, "I would also like to draw your attention to this common-or-garden dog, here, who showed extreme courage in the face of danger." The crowd cheered again, and Stomper tried to look modest, which wasn't easy, especially as Lovely Lucy was licking his ear – the one that remained – and gazing up at him with adoring eyes. "One last thing. Would the earthling known as Shrimp Salmon stand up, please?" Shrimp stood up (even then it was hard to see him). "Shrimp," said Willie, "yon varlet up yonder," said Willie, pointing to the top board, "having finished his confession, needs to be rescued. Perhaps you would oblige?"

"Certainly," said Shrimp Salmon, and then added, "sir," as he started for the pool looking appropriately pink.

"Young man!" said a voice from the crowd. It was the mayor's wife. "Would you do us the honour of coming to our house for tea? I'll open a fresh tin of Co-op fruit cocktail if you like."

"I'm sorry," started Willie, "but I have no time for such trifles. For now I must go."

"OHHHHHHHHHH!" everybody moaned.

Willie waited until sufficient gravity had returned to the grandstand before he lifted off spectacularly with a cry of "Snow and farewell!"

"I say!" called Mr Watkins after him, "I think you mean Hail!"

But Willie hardly heard him as he gazed down at his fans and waved goodbye. He did, however, hear somebody.

His sister called out: "It's Our Willie! I'm sure it's Our Willie, Our Dad!"

"Don't be daft, Our Darleen!" said Willie's dad. "You've never been the same since you had them ears pierced."

"It *is* him!" shouted Darleen, standing up. "If it isn't Our Willie, where is he now then, Our Dad? He were sitting down there at the front a minute ago!"

"Likely gone for a Jimmy Riddle," said Willie's dad.

A moment later Willie had vanished into the blue up yonder.

TWENTY

A Day to Remember

He landed in a cow-pat in the field behind the grandstand, still thinking of the cheers. *Pride goes before the fall* – as Miss Minsky would not have hesitated to remind him had she been there (which she was not, she was still busy enjoying her recovery).

He wiped his boots clean, removed his magic suit and folded it inside-out so that it looked like a battered old sports bag once more, and fastened the zip. Then he clambered over the fence and dropped down into the gents' toilets at the back of the grandstand.

"Where've you been, Our Willie?" asked his dad as he came out.

"Toilets, Our Dad," he said.

"Told you!" his dad said, looking rather smugly at Darleen.

"He was *exactly* like him!" said Darleen, pouting.

"Only his knees, Our Darleen," said Willie's mam. "And his nose. The rest of him were normal."

Willie smiled as he went down the steps to the front of the grandstand.

"You've missed it all again," said Sally as he sat down beside her.

"Missed what?" he asked.

"That Superkid's just been."

"Where?" asked Willie, looking round.

"He's been and gone, cod lump!" said Sally.

"He's saved all the charity money that was going to be nicked. And *I've* won the prize!"

She held it aloft.

"I'm right pleased!" said Willie.

"Everybody is," said Sally, looking round at all her friends.

She seemed to have a lot now. Some of them the same people who'd been calling her Smellygrub all week. And Arnold Buttermouth was coming towards her holding his chocolates out, his teeth flashing like the Blackpool illuminations.

Willie turned away. He went towards the one person in that crowd who didn't look happy – Nigel Spodger. He was standing in the midst of all these smiling people, looking glum. Willie went up to him.

"Cheer up, Nigel," he said. "It's not your fault."

"Eh?" said Nigel. He was amazed that anybody would speak to him after what had happened. "What do you mean?"

"I said it isn't really your fault," said Willie. He took out his packet of mints. "Fancy a mint, Nigel?" he said. "Go on. Take two. It is your birthday, isn't it?"

"Thanks," said Nigel, gaping in amazement. "Thanks a lot, Willie."

"Form a crocodile!" Mr Watkins shouted. "Miss Minsky's class in front."

"Boys and girls in my class may walk together this time, if they wish," said Miss Minsky, blushing as she glanced at Mr Watkins.

Willie started looking round for somebody to walk home with. He knew Sally Mow would be walking back with Arnold Buttermouth, and he'd just seen Shrimp driving off in the police-car.

But a hand touched his elbow and turning round he saw Sally Mow.

"Where d'you think you're off to, Willie Scrimshaw?" she said. "*You're* walking back with me."

"Am I, Sal?" said Willie. "I thought you'd prefer Arnold Butterworth."

"I don't like cowards and cheats," she said.

"How d'you mean?"

"You know nowt, Willie Scrimshaw," she said. "Didn't you notice him yesterday when Nigel came up to me in the yard? He did nowt to protect me, not like you. He just looked the other way."

"I think he was looking for new planets, Sal," Willie said.

"You must've been born yesterday, Willie Scrimshaw!" said Sally. "He was scared to death. And what about him getting all that start in the final?"

"He *did* have a cold, Sal. He kept dabbing his nose in his hanky."

"I'll dab *your* nose in a minute!" said Sally. "First time his nose got wet was when he was blubbing down it because he hadn't won the prize! Even then he had to get a box of chocolates! He's just offered them to me."

"And what did you say, Sal?"

"I told him to stuff them," said Sally. "He wanted to swap the chocolates for my prize but I told him there are some things in life more important than chocolates." That sounded familiar to Willie. "In any case, I told him, that Superkid told me to look out for somebody right brave and reliable," Sally said.

Willie smiled. He couldn't remember saying any of that. "And you think I'm right brave and reliable like, do you?" he asked

"No," said Sally, "but you'll have to do till I find something better. I wish you'd seen Superkid, though, Willie. He were great."

"*Was* great!" Mr Watkins corrected her, as he walked past.

"Who were?" Willie asked her.

Sally told him the whole story as they crocodiled

their way towards Brick Street taking turns at carrying the trophy. "Tall, handsome, ten times better-looking than you, Willie Scrimshaw," she said. "As a matter of fact, the only thing like you was his big nose. I do wish you looked likc him, Willie. I might even fancy you then!"

But although she spoke harshly, she was smiling.

"I try my flipping best!" said Willie, trying to look grumpy and disappointed, but laughing like a drain inside.

"Partners hold hands as we cross this dangerous road!" ordered Mr Watkins when they reached Cemetery Way and as if to set a good example he took Miss Minsky's. She appeared to be still vastly enjoying her recovery.

"Here," said Sally, "give us your hand, Willie Scrimshaw, I might as well see you safely over the road. Flipping heck!" she said as they stepped off the kerb. "I've got a right funny feeling I've held this hand before!"

"Not that I know of," said Willie, smiling secretly. "You must've been dreaming." *Brave Sir William Scrimshaw,* he was thinking, *prepared to escort Lady Sally safely across the crocodile-infested Umbojumbo river.*

Which was how they crossed Cemetery Road. Hand in hand. Sally watching out for flying hearses, and Willie keeping a sharp look-out for crocodiles. By rights, of course, the sun should have been sinking in the west and the birds chirping in the trees, and a thousand baldy-headed fellers should have been playing their fiddles like billio, just out of sight. But that didn't happen a lot in Muckyford.

But at least for the moment there wasn't a hearse in sight (though they could hear one revving-up); it was pie and peas for dinner and in three weeks it would nearly be the holidays; there was only a slightly heavy drizzle and – most important of all – they each of them had somebody's hand to hold on to, someone they loved.

And that, in Muckyford – or anywhere else in this universe for that matter – makes a day to remember.